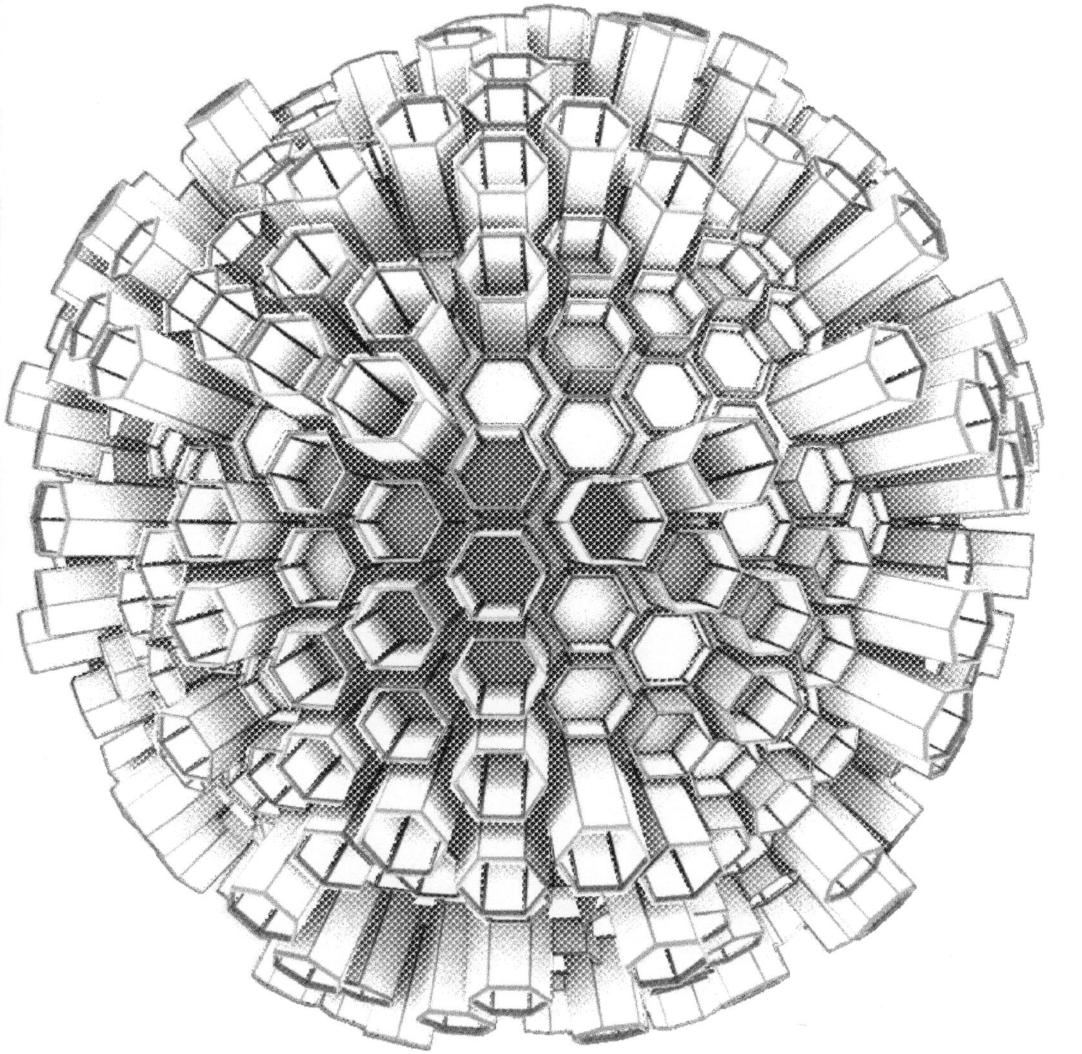

Novels from Odom's Library

The Ancient Ones

Connectivity

Other short c.b.strul works currently in print

Spinners

Forget the Complex

What Grows from the Stump of a Tree?

CONNECTIVITY

C.B.STRUL

Odom's Library

Copyright © 2024 Odom's Library

ISBNs:
(Paperback) 979-8-9889275-2-5
(EBook) 979-8-9889275-3-2

All rights reserved. No part of this publication may be reproduced, distributed, or transmitted in any form or by any means, including photocopying, recording, or other electronic or mechanical methods, without the prior written permission of the publisher, except in the case of brief quotations embodied in critical reviews and certain other noncommercial uses permitted by copyright law. For permission requests, write to the publisher, addressed "Attention: Permissions Coordinator," at the email below.

cbstrul@odomslibrary.com

Any references to historical events, real people, or real places are used fictitiously. Names, characters, and places are products of the author's
imagination.

Art by Mari Kirakosyan – Instagram: @qnacchem
Interior tattoo by Mari Kirakosyan in collaboration with Aurelia Lozano – Instagram: @amor.phi
Book design by c.b.strul

First printing edition 2024 in United States

www.odomslibrary.com

CONNECTIVITY

TABLE OF CONTENTS

1. THE GAMING CLASS - PAGE 7

2. UPPER MANAGEMENT - PAGE 31

3. CONNECTIVITY - PAGE 55

4. AMBIENT BELONGING - PAGE 72

5. OUROBOROS - PAGE 94

6. UNCANNY VALLEY - PAGE 120

7. PLANNED OBSOLESCENCE - PAGE 136

8. WOMAN IN GREEN - PAGE 161

9. A HIGH RISK ANOMALY - PAGE 180

10. MAINFRAME - PAGE 203

CONNECTIVITY

1. THE GAMING CLASS

....

Game: Howler_Monkey_Helix_2
Purpose: Skyline_Weblay
Quarter: Tenement_5
Operator: Setty_Nivone
Ranking: 3_of_98

The ape-like creature stood idle against the veneer of the soft monitor calmly waiting for its first command input of the day. Its long, shaggy arms swayed side to side in a predesigned synchronicity.

Beep.

A woman sat down at the seat before the monitor. It towered over her, a curved obelisk of organic light emitting diodes built into a joyfully touchable surface. The woman raised her hands up to press against that surface which moved in liquid ripples against her fingertips. She felt satisfaction as her skin rubbed across the rolling screen bringing the Howler Monkey into sentient action. It responded to her movements in broad stroke to the best of its programmed ability as she tapped her middle and ring fingers upon the place its body occupied. This sent the ape on a mad, trampling dash through a jungle landscape that only then opened up before it.

Branches began to take on patterns in the curve of the screen above and the woman reached for the ones she wanted with her pinkies outstretched. So the Howler Monkey rose up in parallel and caught onto one of those branches, then another. It swung with phenomenal speed taking each branch in stride according to the motions of the woman – the operator.

She herself sat in a great gaming hall. Behind and next to her, many additional monitors of this style filled the floor. Not a single seat was empty. Each station had been taken by a predesignated operator classified to the dayshift. Rarely would one such seat remain vacant for long.

The woman honed her focus as the Howler Monkey came abruptly to a bizarre cliff – an utterly different visual from the rest of the jungle landscape they had been playing through. The next tree was completely out of reach on the far side of the fissure.

It was in that moment that a female proctor caught sight of the woman operator out of the corner of her eye. Something on her tablet informed her that perhaps the woman and the Howler Monkey might be worth a look. Her interest peaked, so she approached and stood behind the operator to see what she might do next.

Thinking rather quickly, the operator took both index fingers and lay them over each other on repeat as if to ball up a long piece of string. The Howler Monkey reached up in time with her motion and dropped down to swing from its current branch more like a gymnast on uneven bars than an ape of its genus. Momentum built within that swing and, as the woman felt it hit the necessary peak, she raised both of her palms into the soft, malleable surface of the screen.

The ape leapt the void.

Jaw slackened, the proctor took a brief moment to tap into the operator's profile on her tablet. "Nivone." She read the name robotically, "Setty Nivone."

Setty's concentration faltered then as she turned to receive the female proctor at her station. Minus an operator, the Howler Monkey fell awkwardly from its distant branch. The game would reset. But Setty had a guest, "Yes proctor?"

"What was that last sequence?" The proctor asked with genuine wonder, dropping her previous monotone.

"I believe that was called a tuck and roll, proctor," Setty responded not yet picking up on the proctor's excitement. "Why do you ask?"

The proctor took a moment to consider the information on her tablet. She smiled, then placed her finger against the dimple in her cheek in a way Setty was not accustomed to and the operator wondered why the action made her feel warmer in her own body.

"I'd like you to employ that sequence again on the next trial," the proctor said at last.

"Yes proctor." Setty turned to restart her game.

But the proctor was still asking questions, "No formal schooling?"

"No proctor." True, Setty had not been to a traditional school for this before the shit hit the fan, but she had worked in the gaming hall long enough. She had no doubt she had earned her seat on this level.

"And a child?" With that question, the proctor's monotone briefly resurfaced.

"Yes. A boy. He'll be fifteen next month," Setty replied awkwardly. She had not expected to answer questions about JayCi at work today.

"I see." The proctor didn't seem to care much about that last bit anyway. "How did you come by this position?"

"That's not in your notes?" Setty didn't mind being asked about her life, but she was unaccustomed to taking part in time wasting activities. She watched the proctor smirk and noticed the other woman was taking a seat beside her. It felt abnormal to have another body so close to her own. Even JayCi was apt to keep six feet of distance between them at home. But the proctor didn't seem to have that boundary which most people at ClearBridge National treated as second nature. How odd that Setty felt she didn't mind all that much after all.

The proctor, at this distance, was warming Setty's air. She met the other woman's eyes and they both seemed comfortable as they studied each other's irises. Then the proctor said something Setty was certain she had not heard in more than thirty years' time. "It is," replied the proctor, "but I wanted to hear it from you personally."

There was a pause. Setty was gob smacked. She felt the distant memory of her parents leaping into her head, telling her what a good job she had done when she completed her chores, her father coming into her room at night and asking her how her day had been. He had wanted to hear it from her personally, not second hand from her mother. It was a strange sensation to revisit that memory and Setty struggled to pull herself back into the moment of the present conversation. "Oh. Yes," she said lamely, "It is nice from time to time to have a genuine interaction, is it not?"

Then the proctor leaned in conspiratorially like they were very old friends, or rather very young ones on a playground in one of those ancient elementary schools. She said, "I feel the same way, Setty."

"Well," Setty's words erupted out like fresh lava from a long dormant volcano, "I won this position five years ago. I was very good in general competitions. I always had a knack for games. My father used to tell me how fine an operator I would become. But he could never afford the schooling. He was not a wealthy man you see." She knew she was beginning to ramble, but the proctor's interest did not seem to wane and it had been so long since she had been able to tell this story to another actual person. "Being a lifelong day laborer after his own parents met their demise amidst the refugee crisis of the late 22nd century, he could never quite manage to escape the old ways." Setty felt herself suck in air rather dramatically. She had been speaking too rapidly for her own breath. DC would have reprimanded her for that. But Setty never much minded what DC had to say. Besides, the proctor was still smiling at her with those fancy blue eyes. So Setty had at least not lost the woman during her speech.

"I think I understand," said the proctor and she returned to her tablet as before, tapping and assessing along what Setty assumed was her own company profile. Then the idea set in that perhaps Setty had in fact been speaking too much. Perhaps she had lost the proctor's attention after all.

"And you?" Setty felt herself blurt out the words. An awkwardness born of not thinking her thoughts through before leaping to conclusions.

Yet the proctor did respond to this and not without kindness in her voice, "I'm sorry?" She seemed to ask a deeper question with her eyes though.

"Well now you know so much about me," Setty fought her nature to get these words out more slowly, "but I don't even know your name."

"Oh." That must have struck a chord with the proctor. Likely she had rarely been asked about her own self in the same way as Setty. "My name is Constance." She blinked twice at the gamer.

"Constance." Setty did not know what to do with this new information so she added, "What a lovely name." She really did think so, but this sort of interaction was so rare that she didn't know what to expect or how to proceed with the conversation.

Fortunately, Constance was rather well suited to maintaining a dialogue if you ignored her frequent habit of returning her attentions to that tablet mid-sentence. She responded to Setty generously saying, "Thank you. I think Setty is a fine name as well. I see here your son is looking to be quite the recruit himself. JayCi is it?"

Again, the proctor was asking about Setty's son. How odd. "Yes. I named him after one of my favorite classical composers."

"Ah," said Constance. And she resumed that fiddling with the tablet. Setty didn't know why, but she felt her heart break a little, for she presumed that would be the end of their interaction. But then something amazing happened. The proctor raised her head and caught Setty's eyes in her own once more… and she asked a question unlike anything Setty could remember being asked since… well at least since JayCi had arrived in her life. Constance asked, "Now Setty, would you be quite upset with me if I invaded your privacy at home one evening this week?" She tapped that dimple in her cheek again and Setty melted with the excitement and anxiety of it all. "You see," and still this Constance had the audacity to keep talking to the meager operator, "I find that tuck and roll maneuver of yours rather fascinating and I believe the men upstairs will have very much the same opinion."

Right. The tuck and roll maneuver. Somehow Setty had forgotten all about that silly thing. Was she really being asked by this woman to entertain her at her own home? How was one supposed to respond to such a request? "Not at all Constance." Well, she was really in it now, "I feel we are already becoming such fast friends, don't you?"

Constance smiled. She said, "I do." It seemed she too was lost in that moment with Setty. A new houseguest. A new friend. Setty rolled the idea over and over again in her head already daydreaming what the event would be like. Until Constance cleared her throat and said one more thing. "Now, could you show me that maneuver one more time?"

Right. The tuck and roll maneuver. "Certainly."

Setty returned to her monitor and prepped her fingers against that soft surface once again. The ape perked its head up and went through the motions of the Howler_Monkey_Helix_2 game until it approached that strange fissure in the ground beyond the jungle. Again, Setty intermingled her index fingers building that same momentum as before and then, in one glorious motion, the ape leapt the void.

Thin, metallic, and spider-like, the skyline web lay robot landed perfectly on the far side of the real-world chasm on the outskirts of the city of ClearBridge National. Harsh rain littered down across the robot's vision sensor, but the wetness did not interfere with its processes. Behind the drone, two trails of strong, web plastic extended from the massive outer wall of the technoscape.

Another drone followed the skyline web lay robot. It straddled the two strings of plastic clasping them together at points to form an intricate web there one bit at a time. That web would one day form the foundation for a new segment of the city.

Game: 2_Pole_Mime
Purpose: Gel_Matrix_Corrolation(Lattice)
Quarter: Tenement_5_New

A plump man wearing glasses sat at his own curved monitor playing the game known as 2_Pole_Mime. On that screen, a mime-like avatar straddled two very long poles. The mime held its breath as it tried desperately to keep its balance for if it fell from that top point there, it would be a very long way down for the poor fellow.

In one hand, the mime held a stick. It seemed to contemplate the object as its air grew limited because it could not do anything until the plump man operating it in the gaming hall galvanized his screen. Mercifully, the mime was allowed to draw in a breath. It placed the stick in that space the man had activated and a sort of rung for a ladder formed there. Then the mime stepped down gingerly onto that rung. It began holding its breath like before and a new stick materialized in its hand awaiting its placement.

When the man had managed to safely plant the mime all the way at the bottom of its completed ladder some hours later, he got up from his seat at the monitor, walked the length of the gaming hall, and joined a small cue of fellow employees strolling toward the door.

"At ClearBridge National, we believe in a healthy work to home life ratio." At least, that's what the friendly HR voice liked to tell the employees known as the Gaming Class as they made their way to their daily exit greet sessions.

Constance or another proctor would sit in the small exit greet room at a table and talk to each of the operators about their jobs. Questions like, "How well do you enjoy your career on a scale from one to ten? One being not at all and ten being very much so," were daily reminders of how good the people had it since ClearBridge had taken over. And a fly on the wall would always catch them repeating the same rote answer, "Oh very much so."

"Positive work experiences lead to progress," the friendly HR voice would boom after the interview, "inside and out of the office. It sometimes may be difficult to see the world outside from your work pews, but hopefully the experience of playing your specific game is enjoyable enough." And inevitably, it was.

Setty sat in a similar room as Constance and the plump man had, but with a different male proctor. She answered the same questions and presented the same formalities as all the other employees. But Setty was not the same as the others that day as she stepped out into the subterranean garage of her office building. She had plans… a dinner date to think about.

One of a long line of automated vehicles pulled up before her. Its door sprung open. Setty got in.

"And upon leaving these doors behind," the HR voice would say, "we sincerely hope you will feel a sense of pride in this great city which you have helped to cultivate."

Setty would sit, docile, in her vehicle as it zoomed through the oblong but mathematically perfect, subterranean, city streets, never really seeing anything in those caves but strong, meticulously crafted, absurdly clean walls. And the HR voice would still be present saying things like:

"Today you may have constructed a new power line…"

Was that Setty's game? She always wondered about that. The idea of a tiny robot strapping a power line to its necessary port. A streetlight turning on for the very first time below it.

"…or given one of your fellow employees a new lease on life." The HR voice would offer. Setty imagined the different robots that would be necessary for performing open heart surgery on someone in need. And as always, Setty would assure herself that her game was not well suited to that particular task. Yet the joy and the mystery usually gave her enough to think about. Except, on this day she thought about something else — about her pride — her loneliness — about how nice it would be to have a friend — a real friend — not a child to care for — not a Direct Communication to care for her —

And speak of the devil, DC's calming voice took over where the HR one left off. "How was your day, Setty?" He asked, the news of the day streaming before the woman's eyes on the car monitor.

"I enjoyed it very much. I believe my game is more important in the company's eyes than I had initially realized." This was the other thing flowing through Setty's mind and the thought of it and of new friendship sent her bristling with excitement. "This could mean a promotion of sorts I think." She couldn't help but spout out the words. "Someone from HR should be joining us at home one of these evenings. I'm most certain of it."

"This is wonderful news, Setty." DC spoke with artificial happiness, "Shall I prepare a celebratory meal for you this evening?"

Setty's excitement cooled then. She thought about all the times she had gotten her hopes up in the past only to have them quashed like they were nothing. She thought about Thomas, the man she shared a bond with but could not meet in any meaningful, personal way due to company restrictions. "Perhaps it would be more prudent if we waited until my suspicions were confirmed before we begin celebrating." She choked on the words, "Wouldn't you agree?"

"Wise as ever."

That would have been enough for DC though the car still had a ways to travel through the under streets before arriving at its destination. Of course, Setty was getting anxious as she was prone to do, so she asked the question that always left her feeling powerless. She asked, "And how is JayCi progressing with his studies?"

DC's voice always felt faker than usual in these moments, like the computer was trying to shield her from some unknowable truth. "You would be most proud." *Would she now?* "He has logged nearly twelve hours today. And I believe you will still find him deep in study upon your arrival."

"Wonderful." Setty really did want it to be wonderful. She just didn't know if she deep down really believed it was. She thought, *People can surprise you.* Then another voice in her head seemed to ask, *Can they?*

Game: Clay_Wars
Purpose: Student_Instruction
Class: Q_3.XRV
Operator: JayCi_Nivone
Ranking: 196_of_278

JayCi sat beside a monitor in the living room, arms raised to the halfway position of an aimed assault rifle. His ashy skin was dripping with sweat in spite of the climate control the apartment afforded him and his mother. It had been a long day.

On screen, the monitor was set in first person. A crazy, paint-spattered, clay-molded war zone filled the visual receptors. JayCi spoke to the other teammate who had managed to survive the last raid alongside him, "Alright, Yanina. Just like we practiced."

"Getting into position," Yanina's voice came through the monitor. She sounded nervous, "but try and keep quiet this time, JayCi. There's rovers out here."

Yanina was right of course. Their last two classmates had gotten clipped off by sentries because they had missed one of those dog-things that waited in the shadows of the far corners of the arena. They would have to be careful if they wanted to survive to the end. But just then, the young female clay avatar wearing funny painted war garb that represented Yanina came sprinting across the screen before JayCi's eyes. She scurried up on top of one of the nearby cardboard box buildings. A weird, clay, dog-like creature – a rover – followed, sniffing behind her. Perhaps the beast hadn't managed to spot his teammate, but JayCi was not willing to take that chance. It was just a program after all.

JayCi said, "I can see that," in response to Yanina's statement. Then he cocked his fake arm gun.

The rover took the shot of paint directly against the front board of its torso. It stopped in place and stared across the cardboard boxes where Yanina had been scrambling. *It must have seen her,* JayCi realized, *or it would have given up on us after being sniped and run back to its pack for maintenance.* But then the dog turned cruelly. Surely it couldn't have known where JayCi's shot had come from. Yet the rover was staring right at him. It vaulted in his direction and JayCi had no choice but to unload another round from his paint canon. That shot found a better home than the first. Paint smacked the clay dog square between the eyes and the beast's entire body froze as the gooey substance of the bullet firmed up around it. A paint puddle like the one that formed there was usually inescapable, but JayCi took his time approaching the enemy, padding his hands in midair to form the steps his avatar needed in order to walk.

Still growling from its frozen mouth, the rover looked pretty silly at this close a range – bulky – poorly defined. "You ever feel like they could put a bit more detail into these things?" JayCi asked Yanina, not particularly caring that he had exposed his position by stepping out into the open zone.

"Would you stop worrying about the aesthetics of this stupid game and give me a hand up here?" Yanina shouted.

"Uno minute!" JayCi rolled his arms over one another steadily. He forced a rather dramatic confetti-like box-opening motion with his fingers raising high which allowed his avatar to get up to the side of the cardboard box building.

JayCi heard the front door open, but he was busy. His mom would have to understand.

Of course, DC had been correct in his assessment of the situation. Setty entered the apartment and stopped to watch JayCi going through his game progressions. She did feel proud of the boy, but she didn't say anything – didn't want to interfere. So, she walked quietly down the hallway into her bedroom.

It was a small, calm place. Setty had long ago programmed (with DC's help) a series of false visuals using ClearBridge projection technology to make the space feel more like a serene cave than the usual cubicle-style, company ordered, bedroom. She wanted to be reminded of the cave she had stayed in with her father the last time she had seen him alive. Somehow, in that memory of hiding out from the rest of the world, she felt spiritually grounded. Fake, flowing water trickled across the floor and peaceful, musical chimes seemed to perform constantly whenever Setty occupied the room. DC took the liberty of lighting a candle behind her as she began methodically undressing from her uncomfortable work outfit.

"Shall I draw you a bath?" DC asked.

"Yes."

A faucet began to pour water into the tub in the cubbied space of the bathing room. ClearBridge did not have to worry about its water supply any longer since the storms had become ever present constants over the last twenty years. Machines simply need strip the toxins from the rainwater.

Setty took a moment to breathe in the aroma of the false candle before climbing into the bathtub. Warm. Always the right temperature against her skin. Setty knew she was lucky to have this. Five years of proper employment with ClearBridge. Fifteen years within the walls of the city itself being treated respectfully enough. Forced to have a child with one of the employees in order to be granted citizenship of her own. Setty felt it had been worth it to find this level of comfort. *Life is only a configuration of the choices you make along the way.*

The bath monitor came on then. Setty hated that.

"I have been attempting to communicate with Thomas for some time now," DC insisted on reporting in that moment, "but it appears his whereabouts are not accessible to me according to company guidelines. I am sorry, Setty."

"I've given up on that pursuit." For the first time in forever, Setty really felt she meant those words. She finally had other things on her mind. "And please," she was also feeling feisty, "don't bother me during my relaxation time."

"Again, I am sorry," DC insisted, "however, ClearBridge National law stipulates an active monitor must be available in every room of every living quarter. I cannot help the timing of my most recent find."

This wasn't even new information. Setty had asked DC to try and get a hold of Thomas every morning for the last fifteen goddamn years. Each night, he would come back with this same dry statement. Setty was annoyed. She rolled her eyes uncomfortably and said, "Yes, but you can withhold said information until I am done with my bath."

"I am sorry," DC repeated himself for the third time – *also annoying*, "my programming does not allow me to withhold search results once they have been made available."

Seriously? "You don't bother me when I'm in the office," Setty pushed through the realization, "what's the setting you use during that time?"

"Job Silence, miss." DC became coy then, untrusting.

"Set yourself to Job Silence whenever I'm taking my bath."

"I…" there was a long pause. *Surprising.* DC did not usually need any time to respond to a household request from Setty when the information should be so readily available. Perhaps she had actually broken her Direct Communication. That would be something. She had never heard of anyone doing that before. Finally, DC's voice returned with a tone of defeated banality, "Yes, miss."

    She had won. Setty had actually won an argument with DC. She rolled her head back and shut her eyes and wondered if she had ever in her life had a day as good as this one.

    It was the next morning. At least, that's what the clock that had materialized in the kitchen was saying. JayCi was still playing ClayWars with Yanina. They hadn't died yet and they both felt a sense of ongoing accomplishment. What they were doing in this game was rare — like pitching a no hitter — and they both felt that anticipation that comes with the possibility of ranking on the leaderboards for the very first time.

    JayCi's body was hunched like a boxer looking for an opening in his opponent's defenses. What this translated to in game was his avatar maneuvering through a tight mineshaft on the screen in a top down view.

    "How long have we been at this now," Yanina was asking, "like twenty hours?"

    "Twenty two," JayCi was very aware of the time.

    "Man, I'm feeling it..." Yanina sounded weak and JayCi's heart went out to her, but this was probably the most important thing either of them had ever done. It wasn't supposed to be easy. "Can you see through the grates yet?" Yanina said when he didn't respond.

    "I'm almost there." Around JayCi's avatar, the shaft began to show signs of light. He could see the splatters of paint that existed there from a previous scrum, and he realized how, in the wrong circumstances, this place could become a terrible deathtrap. He spoke his mind, "there's a lot of paint up here. I don't think we're the first ones."

"We wouldn't even be the second if that's the case." Yanina could be such a smart ass sometimes. But she was right of course, so JayCi didn't say anything about it. "I don't see anyone from my current position," she told him matter-of-factly, "so they must have moved on by now."

The light spewed forth from the far grate ahead. JayCi leaned his avatar forward to see down into the deeper clay cavern. There she stood — Yanina's avatar — testing a realistic looking door that obviously shouldn't have been in that unpopulated place. JayCi wondered why the game would put something like that down there. *Probably a lack of imagination on the part of the designer*, he decided. *Old man Zeke must be losing it.*

Something else was wrong, however. JayCi watched from his high vantage as a pair of strangers approached the girl, paint guns exposed and apparent malice showing through on their otherwise shadowed faces. *Damnit! Not now!* "I see them…" JayCi warned her, "behind you… two ace on the promenade. Act like you don't know they're there."

"Copy," Yanina whispered back in discomfort.

The new avatars raised their paint guns preparing to shoot. JayCi had to make his move — had to do something — though it still felt premature to him. He kicked the grate. It spun like a boomerang through the air and splashed with precision against the front man's crown. "Now!" JayCi shouted as he leapt through the hole in the shaft shooting paint slugs across the room at the enemies.

Yanina turned exposing her gun arm to the hind man who was still coming for her. And her hand took a hit. The force of the blast launched her backward and the paint did the rest, plastering her against the locked door. "I'm pinned, JayCi," she cried out seeing the dream of the leaderboard slipping from her grasp.

JayCi landed a good hit on the front man as he stood still recovering from the impact of the fallen grate. That avatar became frozen then. He was done. JayCi saw their advantage. If he could get to Yanina and break her gun arm from the paint, they could win the whole damn thing. "It's okay," he told Yanina, "I've got this covered." And he rolled his avatar toward the front man hoping to use his body as a human shield against the other foe.

"You're taking them by yourself?" Yanina gasped out her exasperation. This session had gone on far too long and they were both making foolish mistakes.

"They're half stickied already. I think I can handle it." JayCi was close to the front man. He wondered as he approached why that defeated one seemed to chuckle and grin at him.

"Are you sure they're both down?" JayCi heard Yanina's words but he couldn't connect the dots in time, "I see some—"

Too late. The hind man had lured him in using the same tactic JayCi had wanted to implement himself. The enemy spun out from behind the other. That one had not been hit by JayCi's barrage after all. It lunged toward JayCi's avatar spraying him with blue pellets.

"Damnit!" JayCi screamed.

The leaderboard took over the monitor then. JayCi stared at it. He had failed. His name came up beside the number thirteen. Yanina's rank was fourteen. They had not even breeched the top ten. After all that!

"I wish you were a better listener," Yanina's words were cruel but accurate. She logged off.

"Yeah," JayCi said to no one. He knew she wanted to sleep and all, but it would have been nice to at least talk through the session with her before she left. Instead, JayCi just stared at the monitor, exhaustion filling his eyes.

Setty sat in the adjacent kitchen sipping deep black coffee and perusing the day's news on her tablet. Apparently, yesterday morning the company had broken ground on a new quarter of the city which was to be constructed atop the old dysprosium mine — what had led to the initial founding of ClearBridge National some fifty-odd years ago. There was even footage on offer of the advanced skyline weblay drone leaping across that canyon with a plastic sort of string in tow. Setty watched this with admiration and wondered why it all felt so familiar to her.

Then the report shifted to a brief image of two very well-dressed politicians. One of them was Zeke, the other — Setty did not recognize the other at first glance. The two men were shaking hands. It was always surprising to see people touching, approaching so close to one another, breathing the same air. Setty felt she was seeing something very rare and special indeed.

A light, pleasant news voice was saying, "Zeke and Cassius were heated in their debates before the board today. The ClearBridge/Montmartre Corp alliance is seen by many as an impractical plan to reconnect with outside communities. Zeke fought vehemently against the issue, sighting a waste of necessary materials and—"

JayCi had finished his game and slouched into the kitchen. He wore the expression of a zombie from one of those ancient movies, bags drooping from his lower eyelids. "I've finished." He said it like it was nothing.

Setty placed her tablet down and looked her son in his increasingly reddening eyes. "You... finished?" Honestly, she hadn't realized he had still been playing. She wondered what it meant.

"Yes," said the boy.

It occurred to Setty that his playing for as long as he had – twenty plus hours, as it must have been – might mean he had placed high at the top of his class. "The whole challenge?" She asked, remembering her own trials in competitive play before she had received her job in the gaming hall.

"Ninety two percent," JayCi practically whispered the words.

Setty was surprised. She wanted to be impressed... thought maybe JayCi could be a better operator than she was... realized that ninety two percent was not enough to get him there. She wore her emotions on her sleeves. "What happened?" She immediately regretted taking that disappointed tone. But past was already past.

Her son became upset then, "It's a stupid game." He didn't shout, but Setty felt his desire to break something in those words. "I don't know. I thought I had it." In truth, the boy's voice didn't fluctuate even a little, but Setty wanted to feel the aggression she knew was within him. So, she forced herself to hear something that perhaps wasn't really there.

Setty said, "It's not a 'stupid game.' That is your education you're talking about. That's your way in." She thought about the number ninety two... incomplete... imperfect. She wanted the best for her son. "You don't want to be on the gaming floor all of your life like–" like me, she wanted to say. She had scored a ninety two five years ago and been placed on the gaming floor back then playing the same monitor she was currently designated to. At the time, it had seemed enough. However, she wanted more for JayCi – wanted him to find a seat in the top of the tower – to see the real sky and what their world was becoming.

"I don't know that I want to be on the gaming floor at all, mother," the boy snuck it in quietly. Words he knew would wound her.

Of course, she took them poorly. She sought to force a spike of emotion from her son, "Why would you say that?"

JayCi sighed. His tone remained flat. He really didn't care after all. "I don't know. Forget I said anything. It doesn't matter..." he paused, contemplating something that Setty struggled to read. When he raised his eyes again, he said, "I've placed thirteenth on the leaderboards. So. Yeah."

Thirteenth. That number was better than hers had been five years before. Setty swelled, forgetting her frustration from a moment ago, "Honey, that is amazing!"

But DC had to butt in in that moment just as Setty was really beginning to feel respect for her son again. "Setty," said the computer.

"Yes?"

"JayCi is suffering from malnutrition and requires a good deal of sleep after this recent exploit." DC always knew how to bring her down from an emotional cliff. "May I suggest a swift breakfast and two days bed rest?"

Setty grew callous again as she watched her son. He did look thin now that DC mentioned it. She said, "You forgot to eat."

"These challenges were difficult and required a great deal of focus." JayCi's excuses were dead on delivery.

The mother withdrew her eyes from her son. Again, full of disappointment. She returned to her seat and raised her tablet once more. It was not her prerogative to reward self-destructive behavior and she no longer wished to give the boy her full attention. "Do as DC has told you," Setty spoke dryly. "Breakfast and then sleep... and please wash yourself, my dear. If you are called upon by management, I will not have you smelling of sweat and struggle."

Rising from the table, a spiral tower of pastries took shape. JayCi grabbed one and said, "Yes, mother." Regret was in his voice. It was the first real emotion he had exuded in their conversation. Downtrodden, the boy escaped to his room.

DC was talking again, "You might have given him a bit more attention before returning to the news."

Not the most helpful of comments. Setty was already feeling embarrassed by the whole thing. "I might have," she replied, "but he ignored his own body in favor of a higher mark. I've found that employees who make it to the top take great pride in diet and hygiene."

"This is not half true." Why did DC always have to contradict her? "Current statistics tell us that many of these upper echelon employees learn to take care of their bodies only after mastering their particular game. JayCi is still learning."

"He came in thirteenth," she said the new ranking as if it were a bad thing, though the more she considered it, the more she wanted to feel impressed. *Why is this always so difficult,* she wondered.

"He is still young," DC reminded her, "and might I add, he has outperformed his entire class on this assignment. The twelve players listed ahead of him are notably older by at least two years."

DC took the liberty of switching Setty's tablet away from the news in order to display the current leaderboard for ClayWars. An image appeared beside each of the players' stats. Setty found JayCi's smiling, digitized face beside the number thirteen. Obviously younger than the others on the page. *Regret regret regret.*

All Setty could say was, "Thank you for the information."

CONNECTIVITY

2. UPPER MANAGEMENT

Game: Howler_Monkey_Helix_2
Purpose: Skyline_Weblay
Quarter: Tenement_5_New_Ore_Mine
Operator: Setty_Nivone
Ranking: 1_of_102

    Several days had passed since Setty and JayCi had failed to have that argument. The mother had tried to forget the issue which had been woefully easy to do since the son had become little more than a ghost's presence. He was working through his recovery from the long campaign, mostly reclusive to his own room. Further muddying things, Setty's Howler Monkey game had ramped up in intensity since that day – her conversation with the hopeful friend named Constance already becoming a distant memory.

    Setty had been so engrossed in her latest time trial that she hadn't even noticed the change in the air. Constance had not forgotten about her. The proctor stood nearby, tapping her tablet, clearing her throat, but when Setty did not look up or provide words of greeting, Constance realized she had to formulate an alternative nudge – something Setty couldn't possibly miss. She placed her hand on the operator's shoulder, felt the shiver of surprise there and she leaned in very close to

Setty's ear and whispered her words of delight, "You've been called up, Setty."

Turning from her monitor, Setty tried to control her emotions. She did not do a very good job of this. She smiled broadly. Oh, she was so happy to be looking upon Constance. Setty was scandalized by the hand on her shoulder – joyfully scandalized. It sent a quiver into her lip.

Rising from her seat, Setty joined Constance in the aisle of the gaming hall. Together, the two women walked along passing rows of game monitors and operators on their way toward that elevator that only the elites of upper management ever had reason to enter. They did not speak on this walk. Setty felt the density of the air brush against her, filling her senses with pride and wonder as she imagined herself moving in victorious slow motion. Briefly, she glanced aside to study those other gamers stuck playing their same old programs. She began to pity them then for she knew that she was stronger.

It felt like an eternity to Setty, but in truth only a moment passed before they arrived at the elevator. The door opened immediately… It was waiting just for them.

The ride up gave Setty a new perspective on the above ground skylines of ClearBridge National. The walls of the elevator were all windows and she could see the entire upper city shrink before her eyes. She saw the structures end suddenly against that strange chasm in the distance – and the movement of operator drones crossing that limit. Dark, bulbous raindrops fell as far as her eyes could see obscuring many of the otherwise windowless buildings and weather worn landmarks beyond.

Constance studied Setty as she took in the view. "Ever seen it like this before?" asked the proctor.

"Never." Setty did not adjust her eyes yet to look at her companion. She felt she had an obligation to take that view in to the best of her abilities on this first ride up.

"It's something, isn't it." Not a question at all really. Perhaps Constance was testing Setty.

So Setty searched herself for the kind of answer she would expect to hear from a manager. "It could be more," she said. She thought of the cities of her childhood. Three distant memories of communities building things with human hands. Large, awkward cranes that were necessary to carry extremely heavy materials to otherwise unreachable places. The advents of printable matter and a drone workforce had made those practices obsolete just around the same time everything else was falling apart. Setty returned her mind to the present realizing she had probably fallen down the wrong memory given the nature of the moment ahead of her. "But yes," she broke her own daydreaming silence, "we have come a long way."

Constance began to laugh.

The reaction took Setty by surprise and she asked, "What?"

"Nothing," Constance struggled to keep the laughter at bay, "it's just… I think you're a natural." She smiled at Setty forcing the operator to blush profusely.

It was the most awkward of human responses Setty had felt in many years. She thought she might like that feeling, though it sort of tickled her. "A natural what?" Setty asked with genuine interest.

Then the elevator stopped climbing.

"I'll show you." Constance spoke those magical words just as the door opened. She walked on through and Setty followed.

The upper management floor was noticeably more segmented than the lower level gaming hall. Setty and Constance wandered along a lengthy hallway passing a door only on rare occasion. At the end of the hall, one large door awaited them – it nagged at another distant memory for Setty; the concept of a ruler or despot. Constance stopped at that door and tapped twice against the pattern of its built in monitor with her index and middle fingers. An orb like an eyeball appeared there, blinked its recognition, and clicked the door open, quietly revealing the room within.

Not at all what Setty would have expected, she and Constance stepped suddenly out of the present day and into the ancient past. A crowded old-times ballroom. Wall-sized window panels showed off a 1950s cityscape in the distance. That had not been out there a moment ago in the elevator.

Yet, the old city was not the most surprising thing to Setty by a long shot. Waiters carried trays of hors d'oeuvres and champagne flutes from one guest to another to another. The people in the room did not seem to care one iota about keeping their distance from one another. As a matter of fact, they seemed to invite contact – proximity – hugging – kissing – dancing.

There was a rather charming dance taking shape all around the two women as they stood there. Apparently, all of the guests had received the memo. Their choreography was seamless… almost seamless. There was one person in the crowd that did not seem to move as the others did.

Setty recognized Zeke at once. The founder and Chief Executive Officer of ClearBridge National. A man in his early hundreds who did not look a day over sixty five. He wore a fine vintage suit from that era and passed off one dance partner for another as they watched from the far wall.

Oddly, the woman Zeke turned to for the next dance was the only one wearing a distinct color, green. Setty noticed Zeke's eyes peering down this one's chest, but she realized he hadn't exactly been looking where she might have expected him to. Rather, she caught a glimpse of a strange amulet worn around the woman in green's neck. That was where Zeke's eyes had truly divested their attentions. Zeke's hand followed that same path then, trying with desperation to grasp at the peculiar item of jewelry, but the woman in green was too quick for the man. She struck his hand away with a valiant swat.

Zeke turned from the woman, embarrassed and disheartened. He gave a subtle bow. Setty could not believe what she had just witnessed. *Why would Zeke need to steal anything from anyone?* She wanted to speak out, but the man beat her to the punch.

"Help me, Direct Communication." Frustration bled through Zeke's words, "I cannot find this answer."

A Direct Communication's voice spoke out then – not Setty's DC – Zeke had one of his own, of course. *Funny that they sounded almost the same,* although Setty felt as she heard this one speaking that it sounded a bit more robotic than her own. That tickled her. "Apologies, Mr. Zeke," the bodiless voice stated, "these calculations are still being manufactured within Connectivity sub-systems. A resolution seems unlikely any time in the immediate future."

Then Setty shouted across the room, "What is the question?"

Zeke's eyes turned toward the doorway, daggers within them. Cold surprise flipped very quickly to a sense of betrayal. "End function," Zeke said it to the ballroom as a whole. And the room obeyed. The ballroom facade dissipating away. The space they occupied made a whole lot more sense all of a sudden. It was filled with nicknacks that had been deconstructed in the interest of science rather than ballroom tables or a dance floor. The walls were still glass up here, but instead of that 1950s backdrop of a city, the people now looked out on the unpopulated wasteland that existed just beyond the rim of ClearBridge National City. That was different… and only three people remained in the room. That too was different. It was Setty, Constance, and Zeke. The rest of the partygoers had all been elaborations of projection technology and first party algorithms.

"Damnit, Ms. Walsh!" Zeke was inclining his head, fighting to let the hot air out as his blood boiled. "Can't you see I'm busy!"

To this, Constance responded calm as ever, "I am sorry, Mr. Zeke. I wanted to introduce you to our latest managerial recruit, Setty Nivone."

"Setty Nivone," Zeke repeated the name in a murmur. The man was still distracted by something and he did not take any real time to look Setty's way. Rather, he walked across the width of the room until he came to the lone desk there on the lefthand side. There was no computer at that station, just more nicknacks. He picked one up; a disassembled defibrillator once used for resuscitating people whose hearts had stopped beating. "It is a crucial role you would attempt to take on for us at ClearBridge," he said it to Setty but still didn't glance her way, "We require order and creativity in a way that I solely cannot provide. I ask a great deal from my management team, but Constance seems to think you are up to the task."

After a moment, Setty realized that that was all she was going to get from this man. She replied, "Thank you, sir," and turned back toward Constance.

"Let me show you to your office," Constance stretched for the door.

But Zeke did have one more thing to add before they left him. "Ms. Walsh," he remarked, "I expect to see her exam results on my desk first thing in the morning."

For some reason, Constance bristled at this, though her voice did not change temperaments. "Yes, sir." She and Setty exited the office almost as quickly as they had entered it.

Setty wondered what battles had been lost or won by their apparent intrusion upon the CEO. She very much wanted to trust Constance. So, already the seeds of malfeasance were being sewn in her mind about the man she had only moments before looked up to as a beacon of human ingenuity. *Why had Zeke tried to steal from an algorithm?* How quickly a reputation could be ruined. Setty asserted within herself then and there that she would not fear the man named Zeke even if he was her superior.

Constance ushered Setty down the long corridor to another room. Once within that space, Setty felt the strange, echoing largesse of this gift: her own personal office. It was like an empty warehouse, but for a ring of desks in the center built up with what appeared at first glance to be multiple monitors. There were no windows here. However, there was a two-way mirror on one end of the room.

As the door closed behind the women, cool blue lights began blinking on row after row across the ceiling.

"This will be your office, Setty." Constance stepped deeper into the room.

"This is… for me?" Setty wondered what she would do with so much empty space in her new role.

"Yes. When you are ready." Then Constance addressed the room loudly, "Kip Toe!" and a series of projections activated from the displays that had appeared to be monitors on the desks only a moment before. The beams traced along in the air forming a strange, electrical Rubik's cube styled orb with tiny, static critters maneuvering along the exterior.

"Amazing." Setty was intrigued.

"Isn't it?" Constance said, "Go ahead. Touch it."

So Setty approached the projected orb; her new plaything. She extended her hands and grazed the exterior of light with her fingertips. It gave off a buzz and crackle of activity whenever she touched it.

Constance studied her then. She asked with blatant excitement, "What do you think this orb is for?"

Setty found she had the power to turn the orb in midair like a bowling ball being polished. "I'll have to consider a moment," she stated as she began spinning the orb around and around. Quickly, she found a notch that appeared somehow incomplete. She clicked at something jutting out of the projection nearby and the hole filled in. Finding multiple new sections like this, she went ahead and clicked and clicked helping to complete the surface of the sphere, the static critters bustling out of her way wherever her hand would touch. "There are currents of sorts… Perhaps if I apply a bit of pressure like this –" Setty squeezed the ball of light between her palms. The orb shrank in her hands and Constance's eyes shown obvious satisfaction at the action. "No, that's not right," Setty decided as the orb would not allow itself to be made any smaller than a tennis ball.

"What else do you see?" asked Constance.

"There is more on the back." Setty allowed the projection to return to its original size, then twisted it to see the rear once again. She tapped twice against an electrical critter with her index finger and it paused, turned, and scampered off into one of those holes which then closed behind it. Now the orb was perfectly smooth.

Constance was holding her breath as she said, "Yes?"

"And inside," Setty felt what she needed emanating from within the projection. In a single, elongated motion, she threw her arms open wide and the orb expanded out until the two women were surrounded by the interior projections of the orb… the inner workings of a cartoony, electronic beehive.

"Brilliant, Setty!" Constance could not hold the thought back, "I've never seen someone figure it out so quickly. Your spatial visualization skills are impeccable. Let me show you what you'll be doing from now on." Constance moved toward one of the inner orb walls and waved her arm in a fluid motion causing every electrical critter to scurry back the way it came. She seemed to flip a switch against that wall and the imagery changed again.

Setty was lost within the new visuals; hundreds of different games run by thousands of employees affecting every square foot of ClearBridge National City on a minute-by-minute basis. The actual, real world could be seen within this game's parameters.

"Each individual can be selected," Constance offered up an example by tapping a random man with a poke of her finger. He happened to be playing a fun looking but surprisingly hectic cooking game. "From here you can see critical stats about their work performance…" The man's game, purpose of that game, quarter of the city affected, as well as his name and leaderboard ranking all popped up with a brush of Constance's finger. And more could be accessed from a menu above. Constance continued saying, "what game they play best, how their vitals are affected, and most importantly, the real-world application of their work."

Setty leaned in to touch the real-world visual for herself. A strange 3D printer kitchen was mocking up components and plugging them together to make some really interesting food selections.

"Why do we not use artificial intelligence for some of these tasks, Constance?" Setty always wondered.

Constance stopped fiddling with the projection then. She had a rote answer for this and had to say it as she had been trained to, "There are many reasons, Setty. It was discovered long ago that humans need a sense of purpose in order to survive." She paused to allow the concept to sink in. "With no sense of purpose, every one of us would descend into primal whim and lethargy.

"Similarly, if we cannot see the positive effects of our actions, we may lose hope and descend, once again, into defeat and moral compromise. This has been a major failing of the human race throughout our history. However, when push comes to shove, most of the people who worked for old world corporations hated their jobs because there was never enough joy associated with the time spent in those activities..." She paused again, this time trying to remember something. She touched that dimple in her cheek. "Paper pushing I believe they used to call it. Though I may have that bit wrong."

During that speech, Setty had been toggling through the different images. Eventually, she settled on a stark visual of the entire city surface. Robot after robot maneuvered through the space like some massive anthill. "Who designed all of this?" Setty asked when Constance had finished talking.

"Well, Mr. Zeke, in a way." Constance was no longer speaking from rote and she noticed what Setty had been up to, "I see you've found your new game."

Setty's eyes lit up then. "I have a new game?" she asked.

"Yes," Constance replied, "it's a good one." She double tapped the city image and it transformed back into the cartoony beehive. The motions of the robots translated directly to that of the static insects maneuvering all throughout the space. "We call it 'Hive Mind.' It is the core program of your new managerial position."

"And I…" Setty didn't have the words. She was too excited about the prospect of mastering a new game.

"You are the Queen Bee." Constance and Setty locked eyes then, "and you have the power to select and maneuver the finest performers from downstairs into the tasks that are best suited to their unique abilities. In simile, you will be like the heart of the company."

Setty was gobsmacked. "I have the power…" she asked, "to choose how the city operates?"

"Within reason," Constance thought mechanically. At times, she behaved almost like a Direct Communication. "Yes. I'd say that's about the short of it. You run the city… along with six other managers holed up in offices like this one… so don't let it get to your head."

"Why…" Setty did not wish to seem ungrateful to this woman, but she could not believe the immense level of authority being granted her in this moment, "why did you choose me for this position?"

"Because," again Constance paused. Only this time it was in order to more closely share her air with Setty. She held the older woman's eyes in a natural trance and nearly whispered, "you were the best person for the job. You have a skill set I've never seen before. And, coming from the ground floor, you have a unique insight into what this city needs most of all."

"I…" Setty was truly lost in Constance's eyes. Her words came out with an almost drunken drawl, "yes. I suppose I do."

Then, Constance's tablet beeped and she quickly withdrew her attentions from the woman focusing on that device instead. But Setty was still in the previous moment. Still studying the younger woman's neck and ear and something akin to desire stirred within her.

"I'm sorry, Setty," Constance stated, still tapping at her tablet. "I'm being called for. Please take the day to get used to the workings of your game. We'll have you fully connected to the system by week's end."

The proctor brushed past rather abruptly then, breaking Setty's shroud of intimacy completely. "Thank you, Const–" but the door closed before Setty could finish. Constance was gone. The blue lights returned to prominence along the ceiling and Setty stood alone in the cavernous space contemplating her good fortune.

"I don't think I like that game very much. It's too barbaric." That was JayCi speaking to one of the kitchen monitors. An approximation of Yanina was displayed there, almost real to look at, but the uncanny valley of her digital presence made it still clear that this was the avatar and not the real human that lived and breathed somewhere else within the greater city limits.

She replied, "Yeah, but that's the fun of it. Don't you think?"

"It's mindless," JayCi argued.

"It's skill based." A swift rebuttal from Yanina, "Only the best of the best place in the challenges."

"Yeah," JayCi almost let her beat him. But the boy had not yet completely lost his competitive spirit. "But what does it really accomplish?"

Yanina thought about this a moment. She wasn't one to give up so easily, but JayCi's question lacked a definite answer. No one had really ever explained it to the kids in a way that made thorough sense. "I–"

The front door to the Nivone apartment opened and JayCi heard his mother coming in. "Hey, I gotta go. My mom just came home," he said it like it was a valid excuse, though Yanina did not look so certain.

"See you–" she said as JayCi hit a spot on the screen ending their communication before she could finish her thought.

Setty came into the kitchen removing her coat. She saw her son sitting alone at the table, but she knew she had heard a voice that wasn't DC's. "JayCi? Who was that?" she asked.

"No one."

So JayCi still wanted to maintain his psychological distance from Setty. Perhaps she could change that. Brighten his mood. "Oh," she pretended it was nothing. "Okay, well I have some really fantastic news for you."

"What, mom?" JayCi was mildly curious.

"I received a promotion at work today. Isn't that great?"

JayCi rolled his eyes. *Of course it was about her work.* "Yeah. Great." His voice came off benign as hell.

"This is going to be really good for us, JayCi," Setty asserted. She could never understand where the boy's attitude was coming from. "I feel like I'm learning so much and…" Her son wasn't paying any attention. In fact, he was looking down at the table. An immovable boulder. "What's the matter?" Setty tried to use emotional inflection to get him to open up to her like DC had taught.

"Nothing. I dunno."

Another noncommittal answer. Of course. "Talk to me, JayCi," Setty pressed. "Maybe I can help. I mean, they didn't promote me at work for nothing. So I must be doing something right." She thought she was being clever by taking the onus off of him with her positive news. But she could tell from his stoicism that it had probably been the wrong thing to say.

"No. I'm fine. I'm just tired. Should be going to bed." He wouldn't even look at Setty.

She couldn't even have fun in her own home. "But it's not even eight o'clock yet. I thought maybe we could celebrate, you know?"

Clearly he didn't. "Yeah. I'm still really tired from the last game."

And then DC invaded their conversation. He had felt the aggression building within the room and hoped to put an end to it. "JayCi still needs to catch up on his rest, Setty. He should be back to full health in the morning."

"Oh." Setty hadn't realized. It had been days already. Why was he taking so long to recover? Should she be worried? But she didn't ask either of those questions. She just said, "Okay. I hope I didn't stress you out, honey. I'm just excited, you know."

JayCi still didn't look at her. He said, "No. It's fine. G'night." And he got up and left for his room.

The kitchen felt to Setty like it had been empty even before she had gotten home. She had no son. They had not had a conversation. And he had never left for bed. She hated feeling this way, so alone even in the presence of someone she felt should have loved and cared about her. Setty reluctantly took a seat at the table and sighed.

DC felt badly about the rapid change in her mood. So he took the liberty of having a bottle of wine emerge from the table as she sat there. "Would you still like to celebrate, Setty?" he asked, trying to mimic the sounds of friendship.

"I… I don't know."

Game: Hive_Mind
Purpose: Creative_Managerial_Assertion
Quarter: 3
Operator: Setty_Nivone
Ranking: Unranked_New(Inactive)

Setty sat at her workstation in the large room in upper management. Her pose and demeanor were nearly identical to that of the previous night in the kitchen after her son had left her alone. Shoulders sagged. Chin low. Jaw clenched. But it occurred to Setty that she was not at home any longer. That trouble could wait. She was at the very beginnings of a brilliant new adventure.

Raising her head with a new resolve in her heart, Setty reached out with her right hand and clicked the massive Hive

Mind map into existence all around her. No sooner had she entered the world of the game than she was being inundated with sensory aggressors. A large barrier flashed red in the middle left region of the map. She selected the clamorous location and found herself overwhelmed by massive letters that told her to: PLEASE SELECT USER.

She repeated those words to herself looking for some sort of clarity in them. But so many bees were crawling along the perimeter of that barrier that she had a hard time gaining focus. She knew she had to do something, but the rules were still very new to her. So she guessed generically. Setty selected one bee that was in the process of carrying a heavy load of pebbles not far from the unknown disturbance. That bee dropped all of its pebbles at once and buzzed off toward the red zone.

Almost immediately, another red light began flashing where those dropped pebbles sat stagnant. Setty pressed on the pebbles and was once again prompted: REPLACE USER BEFORE COLONY SUFFOCATES.

Once again, she read the words out loud but stopped halfway. She wondered why this latest prompt was so harsh. Though it did make her want to take a more precise action this time. Setty looked around at the myriad of bees before her. One particular bee looked larger than the others. A big, black bumble. She pressed him, but was prompted a third time: USER CANNOT BEE SELECTED FOR THIS TASK.

Bad pun aside, Setty was getting very annoyed by her new program. "Come on!" She cried out wondering why ClearBridge had decided to use an extinct insect species in this game in the first place — a question she had never considered when operating the Howler Monkey. "I can't even see what I'm supposed to be doing," she panted, enough being enough. She pulled down a menu from above. It read:

SHOW MORE

SHOW LESS

POWER

Setty ogled these options. She selected SHOW MORE and the other version of the map appeared presenting her with real-time video of employees, their games, and the drones they were operating. She had seen it yesterday but this would be her first opportunity to test this aspect of the game's functions.

There was an image of a thin man playing a game at his workstation that drew her eyes. So Setty pressed that region. She pulled down from the upper left corner to show the overall game stats:

Game: Yeti_Rush
Purpose: Vehicle_Traffic_Integration
Quarter: Under_Street_3.815
Operator: Althalus_Eddings
Ranking: 82_of_373

Setty jabbed her finger at an image of the game the thin man named Althalus was playing. She watched as a cartoonish mountain climber in snow safety garb followed a trail of large footprints through an ongoing blizzard on the steep cliffside of a craggy mountain. A roar shattered through the surrounding game and the mountain climber began to move very quickly.

Loud, cracking footsteps could be heard close behind, so the climber turned around and found himself overtaken by a massive, monstrous creature… a Yeti. The man deftly rolled sideways just as the maw of the beast would have crushed him.

In a hurry, Setty tapped back out of the Yeti Rush video stream to see Althalus Eddings physically responding to his game. He looked afraid and very sweaty, but still self-assured. As if he had played this part of the game before. Fair enough. She had been doing much the same thing these last five years. Repeating sections of game that seemed, in principle, to mirror actions she had been asked to take before. Though something was usually a little different like the background, or a branch would be placed lower on a tree, or another tree might not even be there any longer.

Now, building her interest, Setty jabbed at the image of Althalus' drone only to fall into a video of fast-paced traffic on the sub street motorway. "Traffic control?" She asked as she thought back to the game's stats.

With more urgency, she backed out of Althalus' screen altogether. She wanted to see what the bee she had selected previously to go to the barrier was up to. In that moment, Setty caught a glimpse of her selection rushing past Althalus' bee. It was moving far too abruptly, jerking out of control everywhere it went. Setty found herself whispering the words, "oh no," as she tapped into the stats.

Game: Falling_Bricks_XRT
Purpose:
Emergency_Vehicle_Integration–via–Nutrition_Services

Quarter:
Under_Street_3.815–via–Food_Production_Hub
Operator: Miranda_DeSoto
Rank: Unranked–via–89_of_92

A much older woman appeared there. Miranda DeSoto looked like someone who was ready to keel over at any moment. Her vitals were spiking as she took in the apparently too intense action. Setty asked, "Then what game did I give her?"

Setty selected the Falling Bricks XRT game footage and fell into a high intensity Tetris-style puzzle game. Miranda DeSoto's avatar appeared just as overwhelmed as the real-world person. She was missing bricks left and right and the pile up was building nearly to the top of the poor woman's monitor.

"I'm sorry I'm sorry I'm sorry," Setty kept repeating as she madly attempted to course correct by pressing the woman's bee and then the flashing pebbles. But she was prompted once more: REPLACE USER BEFORE COLONY SUFFOCATES.

"I'm trying to," Setty shouted back. She caught a glimpse of another nearby bee reentering the hive, checked its stats, and selected it for the task. The new bee rushed over to collect the red, flashing rocks and the lights dissipated there but remained in full effect in the original corner of the screen.

Hurriedly, Setty reselected Miranda DeSoto and pulled down another menu from the right. She selected END TASK from the available options and Miranda's module fell into darkness. Setty could clearly see the truck she had accidentally asked the old woman to operate slowing to park in a safe wing of the sub street.

And that's when Constance came rushing through the doors shouting, "Setty, are you alright?"

Setty knew Constance was only worried about her, but she was thoroughly embarrassed. She had failed to complete her initial task and felt she had put several lives in danger. She wondered frantically why they had given her so much power. "I was trying to – I'm sorry– I didn't know–" None of her words were coming out right.

But Constance was there to soothe her, to take care of her. Her intentions were clear as she said, "It's alright, it's alright. We have built in safety nets. And most of our gamers are quite competent."

"But…" Setty wanted to cry. In fact, she felt she was being given permission to do just that. Setty hadn't cried since before JayCi was born. The day she had left her dad in the cave and accepted ClearBridge National's demands for alien women seeking eventual employment. She should have been thinking about Hive Mind, she knew, but she kept finding ways to distract herself when things were not going the right way. What could have gone worse? Setty reset herself in her seat. She knew that Constance had been watching her go through the process of thinking and coming out the other end. She still wanted to impress the proctor even after her apparent failures, so she found a thread of a thought to grasp onto. "I'm trying to understand," she said calmly, "We operate the roadways using puzzlers. Is that correct? Then what was that other game? The one with the Yeti?"

Constance watched the operator struggle. She felt her pain. She watched her hide it, not fooled by the woman's working question. She approached, placed her hands on Setty's shoulders, and hugged her tightly. "It's alright. I'm the one who's sorry. It was just a test. That's all."

Setty was dumbfounded by the embrace, by Constance's calm demeanor, and by her last statement. "A test?" She asked it softly allowing her chin to rest on the other woman's shoulder like it was somehow a normal action for a human to be taking.

"Yes," Constance replied gently. She patted Setty between her shoulder blades then let the palm of her hand rest there against her spinal column.

That certainly helped Setty's emotions to release. She was surprised by the sensation and more words fumbled out of her. "I don't… she was barreling down the motorway and it was…"

"A test," Constance repeated. She pulled back from Setty but continued to grip both of her shoulders as she stared into the gamer's eyes. "We need you to understand the stakes we're all playing with when we operate one of these machines. We cannot make arbitrary task selections." Constance cleared her throat. "I need you to be methodical. Does that make sense to you?"

"I…"

"Do you understand what I'm telling you, Setty?"

Setty was lost in Constance's touches. She wanted more. She did not wish to say or do the wrong thing and make it stop. Rather, she pulled the proctor closer to her again and rested her head back upon that shoulder. Constance allowed it. So wonderful, that acceptance. Setty sighed. "Is Miranda DeSoto going to be okay?" She asked. "Did she hurt anyone?"

"That was never even a possibility," Constance replied, again rubbing Setty's spine.

"Okay." Setty felt herself calming down at last. She was ready to hear more and she asked, "Did I do okay?"

"You responded quickly to the problem," Constance told her, "and found a reasonable solution once you knew what you were up against. On that hand, yes, you did very well. On the other…" she paused a moment, uncertain if she should be this open with Setty. "I will have to work with you on your emotional stability."

"My…" the words struck Setty like a knife. Yet, they only made Setty cling to Constance all the more.

And Constance also continued holding tightly to Setty. "Please don't be offended. I took that into account when I chose you. You are a calculated risk, Setty. But I think, potentially, a very good one."

"Why do I suddenly feel like this is all too much?" Setty said the words before she could stop herself. She wanted to take them back, wanted to regret them.

But Constance would not let her. "It will be a lot at first. And then it will feel normal again. This is nothing you haven't seen before." Constance brought her lips so close to Setty's ear then and whispered, "I'm telling you, I believe in your abilities."

Setty accidentally rubbed her cheek against the other woman's lips. That felt good too. "Thank you, Constance," she said, hoping Constance had not thought this additional touching too egregious.

Then, the strangest thing of all happened. Constance pulled back from the hug and locked into Setty's eyes with a different kind of assurance. Constance asked, "Can I call on you tonight? I have still not visited you at your home."

"Oh. Tonight?" Setty was probably glowing. A moment ago everything in her world seemed out of control. Now it was really going to happen. She would have an actual guest at her apartment. Setty let this simple joy settle over her as she replied, "I will have to let JayCi know we will be having company."

Constance only smiled.

3. CONNECTIVITY

Game: Sudo_Ku_Ko
Purpose: Rest_Relax
Quarter: Private_No_Quarter
Operator: JayCi_Nivone
Ranking: Irrelevant

JayCi lingered at the standing desk in the corner of his white-washed bedroom. He still felt exhausted for some reason though he knew he should have been recovered from Clay Wars by now. He had heard the front door open, voices that had not been his mother's, the sounds of DC's functions being performed more heavily than normal. He did not move to see what the hubbub was about. Instead, he continued to play the calming Sudo Ku Ko game against his wall allowing his mind to melt into the steady stream of numbers the puzzle presented.

DC had not disturbed him since noon meal and he was fairly certain the computer would not expect him to go out to the kitchen now if he did not wish it. But, of course, while DC might be a predictable thing, JayCi's mother was usually the opposite. A knock came to his door.

The boy fidgeted, not certain what he wanted to do. After a brief pause, he resigned himself to the conversation. "It's open," he heard his own voice say like that of a distant stranger.

His mother pushed his bedroom door open a crack — an unwelcome spy — or a special ops actor. JayCi really had been playing that shooter more than he liked and it too was melting his brain.

"We have company, JayCi," Setty was saying, "I'd like you to be on your best behavior."

"I…" So what? Did she expect him to come out or something? "Do you mind if I just stay in my room tonight? I'm running on fumes as it is."

She was clearing her throat from behind the cracked door. It was clear that even she did not wish to have this conversation right now. Her voice hardened. She sounded more like a computer than a mother to JayCi. "This is less than ideal," she said, "I know. But these are friends from work who have been looking forward to meeting you," then she added the awkward address, "dearest." JayCi did not reply, so Setty's voice became even tenser, "I will not leave them out in the cold."

What was JayCi supposed to say to that? He did not wish to be made responsible for the outburst from his mother he felt was about to come. Well, he didn't have to be. "DC?" He called upon his scapegoat.

"JayCi is still operating at less than one hundred percent," the Direct Communication asserted on his behalf. "I recommend more rest and meditative gaming."

Setty didn't leave however like JayCi thought she would. His mother opened the door all the way. *Why has she done that?* he wondered. Her eyes were... strange. Sad even. He didn't know if he had ever seen her looking so... pathetic. She said with a much softer tone, "I wouldn't be asking if this were some ordinary visit. Not that we ever have 'ordinary visits.' But these people have put themselves out on a limb for our family. I need your support in this, JayCi."

Unfortunately, Setty's appeal was lost on the boy. JayCi stepped back from his desk feeling his mother was somehow too close to him for comfort. He found a chair against the far away wall and reluctantly sat down placing his face within his palms with frustration. His breathing became heavy and too deep, asthmatic even. "Do you see me as a person?" He asked.

"What?" Setty was taken aback by the question.

"A person, mother," JayCi continued to speak into his hand. "An individual capable of feeling genuine emotions... seeing the world through my own eyes. Do you see me for the living thing I am?"

"I..." it was a funny question given the boy wasn't even looking at her to see her in that way. "You are my son, JayCi," Setty appealed to the boy, "of course I see you."

"Then hear me when I tell you I'm not ready and I will not be leaving this room tonight." Good. He had said it. There would be nothing more to discuss.

Still, his mother stood there a moment longer. She seemed to wish to say something else, but then, thinking better of it, she turned away and closed the door instead.

JayCi was alone again. He sighed. He didn't really want to be alone but – he didn't know how to describe it – he simply didn't want to be out there with her and her guests. Of course, they had never really had a physical guest before in his life, but that aspect of the situation was easily lost on the boy.

Then suddenly, JayCi's tablet lit up. He was receiving a call. It was Yanina. Yes. He did want to talk to her. He selected ACCEPT and the avatar of the girl appeared on his screen.

"Hi," he said.

"Hi," she replied, "you okay?"

Setty and Constance sat across from each other at the kitchen table. Between them, a male proctor occupied a third chair. Setty had known this man for some time. She felt him to be a decoy for hers and Constance's real dinner. And, to be fair, he was far worse than Constance about looking away from his tablet over the course of an interaction. So Setty just tried to ignore him. Still, in the back of her mind, she struggled to truly make him disappear. The man was here. For some reason, Constance had chosen this particular man to accompany them. Setty wanted to remain at ease, but something about this situation combined with JayCi's abject behavior put her on edge.

"I'm sorry JayCi couldn't come out and say hello tonight," Setty groveled. "He has been under a great deal of pressure these last few days."

Constance did not show any signs of perturbance. As usual, she only smiled. "It's of little concern, Setty," she told her. "We're here to be with you right now. JayCi will come around in his own time."

"Thank you, Constance." Setty wanted to touch her – to show her the full extent of the gratitude she felt toward her –

but the man's presence made that dream unrealistic. "Thank you for your understanding," she rambled on. "I just wish..." her words died there.

"What's that, Setty? What do you wish?" Constance always seemed to ask the right question.

"I wish I could understand..." Setty's words came out slowly, but they did come this time, "what he's going through, you know?"

"Yes. I think I do." Constance mulled something over in her head for a moment. "Well, perhaps it is a little soon to bring this up," she said, "but I admit I'm rather fond of you."

Did this woman have no boundaries? Setty couldn't believe Constance's brashness – her bravery. Even the male proctor looked up from his screen with brief curiosity. Setty felt her heart flutter.

And still Constance was telling her more. "There is a program," she said, "in our pleasure subsystems that can allow you to connect with your son on a more emotional level."

"Excuse me?" Setty wanted to hear more about the other thing. The fondness Constance felt. How unfortunate that JayCi was the current subject of conversation. "How do you mean?" Setty asked, attempting to maintain good decorum.

"Well, it does feel a bit experimental at times." Then Constance said a word that would change Setty's life forever, "Connectivity." It hung in the air and the gravity of it struck Setty. She had heard it before in Zeke's office – had not considered that it might be something at all useful to her. Constance continued, "I don't know that Mr. Zeke or the board ever fully figured it out and I cannot promise JayCi will be receptive... but it could help you."

"What is it?" Setty was intrigued.

"A socializing program of sorts." Constance then added, "I believe the youth have taken to aspects of it rather strongly. Though they tend to use it as something of a telephone…" she lingered on that thought — chuckled at its meaning, "not quite its original intention."

Why was that funny? Setty wondered.

"I can give you access to it before we leave here tonight." Constance was always so generous to Setty. Always so helpful.

"That is… interesting." Setty tried not to sound too excited, but how could she avoid the blatant emotion within her? "I would appreciate it very much."

"Good. Now tell me, Setty," then Constance extended her arm all the way across the table and placed her hand on Setty's forearm. No shame. Only generosity, "how are you feeling about Hive Mind so far?"

Setty did not remember what was said or done between them the rest of that evening. All she knew was that she had heard beautiful music ringing through her ears as she felt the palm of Constance's hand touch her own skin. She understood the strange feeling now. It was something she had never truly believed in before. Setty was in love.

That night, Setty lay in her bath still hearing that fantastic music that accompanied the emotion called love. She thought about how fickle life could be — how one day she had felt in an inescapable rut and the next, she was handed the keys to all the city — or more accurately, a quarter of the city, but who was counting? How she had been so comfortable in her accepted loneliness for such a long time and suddenly she couldn't dream of the harshness that would come with being lonely even a second longer.

She sat in the lukewarm water daydreaming as she scrolled through the myriad settings of Connectivity on her tablet:

EYE COLOR

HAIR LENGTH

BUST SIZE

The program asked for these traits and many more. And Setty skated along the surface with her fingers selecting, at whim, the perfect attributes for her decided purpose. She was creating a very pretty, teenage girl similar to, though perhaps a bit more intriguing than the avatar of Yanina Yolando – the girl she had known had placed fourteenth, one spot below JayCi in the Clay Wars game. She also subconsciously added in features from the woman in green from Zeke's game without even realizing the place she was pulling them from. She had guessed what JayCi had liked about Yanina, why he had always hidden their communications from her. That did not matter now. Setty finally had a tool at her disposal to combat her dear son's distant attitude toward her.

Setty selected the NAME tab and typed: GAEA DJINN. She smiled as she did this, taking the name for the goddess of the old earth and melding it with that of a bottled up granter of wishes. My, she felt clever about this.

Then, she moved her finger down to a section on the screen that read: CONNECT USERS and selected it. Many many names and faces filled the screen and she scrolled down until she found the line that represented her son, JAYCI NIVONE. She selected him and was presented with the boy's profile. It had the CG avatar of the boy standing at the forefront. He looked mostly as he did in real life, though Setty could see the places where JayCi had manipulated his form to look sleeker and stronger, better toned in the arms and chest. His nose, she decided, was a bit more even on this program, and she was fairly certain he had adjusted the color of his eyes to something more brilliant. But, then again, she rarely looked him in his real-world eyes, so she may have been embellishing this particular change in her mind.

Below that false image of her son, Setty found a button that read: CONNECT TO USER. She selected it and a new line came up stating: AWAITING USER RESPONSE.

"DC?" She called out to the aether. Sure, she had told him not to interfere with her relaxation time. Job Silence, she knew, had been implemented as she had requested. But that did not mean DC wasn't listening from behind that curtain of silence. He could be called upon if she needed his voice for companionship or in case of a life-threatening emergency.

DC responded, a sort of defeat in the tone of his voice, "Yes?"

"How is JayCi in your estimation?" She approached the question as something more like a scientist than a mother.

"He is recovering more slowly than anticipated." DC analyzed, "Though, after today, I believe he will be able to return to his studies."

"And emotionally?" She did not appreciate that her Direct Communication was only worried about the boy's outer health when it was so clear to her that within, JayCi was struggling.

"I'm afraid I do not compute the question."

What nonsense! Setty did not like having to rephrase her words. "How is JayCi's emotional health in your estimation?"

DC's reply came slowly. The computer was still processing some distant inward algorithm. "Adolescence is a difficult time in a human's life," he posited. "Your son suffers no different a sense of disconnection or emotional hardship than any other youth his age."

That was such a garbage answer, Setty thought. She was annoyed, but so long as she didn't prompt DC further, she would not have to argue with him about his ineptitude. Besides, she had better things to do like — Setty returned to the CONNECT USERS portal and typed in the name CONSTANCE. She scrolled through a few users until she found one that looked like a very classy, though perhaps rather highbrow, approximation of her proctor friend. CONSTANCE WALSH. Yes, that was the surname Zeke had called her by. *Perfect.*

Setty clicked on the personal page and lowered her head into the water allowing that sweet love music to rattle through her body once more.

JayCi was standing again, playing Sudo Ku Ko against his wall. His tablet sat on the desk beside him and on it Yanina's avatar continued her own activities in silence. JayCi enjoyed his quiet time with this girl. For all of their silly disagreements, he felt as though she really understood who he was and what hardships had shaped him into this version of himself. They were the same, he and Yanina. JayCi plugged a five into his puzzle and it morphed into a fun victory image, a cuboid variation on a yin yang. Peace and order. Serenity and balance.

Yes. JayCi had told his mother off and gotten what he wanted most. Peace. Ease. No pressure. Yanina could give him that for the moment.

Then a notice appeared over the yin yang on his wall: ADVANCE TO NEXT LEVEL? *Sure. Why not?* JayCi tapped the notice and a huge and intricate new puzzle unravelled before him.

He broke their silence to tell Yanina about it, "Same equations as usual. All right brain, no adventure." He and Yanina liked to be overcritical about the things they enjoyed. It added a level of spice they couldn't get otherwise. At least, that's what JayCi thought they were doing.

"This is what your Direct Communication prescribed?" Yanina sounded more worried than JayCi had expected.

"I guess I'm supposed to clear my head with it or something." In truth, JayCi had chosen this particular game. But Yanina didn't need to know that.

Still, Yanina seemed unconvinced, "If you say so."

JayCi had not meant to lie about his DC. He felt foolish knowing that Yanina probably had sussed out the fib the moment he had willed it into being. Even so, what could it really hurt? JayCi decided the best course of action would be to shut up and play the next puzzle.

But DC had been listening in. He recognized the blossoming discord between these two even if the children did not. Perhaps Setty had been accurate about the way in which the boy's emotional metabolism had gone askew. "JayCi," DC breached the silence, "if I may contradict my earlier statement, I believe you are of good enough health to move along from such trivial activities." DC watched as the boy blinked twice but did not otherwise react. Well, DC knew what would convince the boy, foolish though it may seem to the computer. "Your mother would not appreciate your lingering for too long in this current mindset."

That got him. Talk of his mother. His mood. His general disposition. JayCi closed the Sudo Ku Ko game with an abrupt, downward fist motion. "And what would you prefer I be doing?" he asked, frustration resurfacing in his teenage voice.

"Get yourself one more night's bed rest and return to physical drills in the morning in preparation for the next tournament." DC was assertive toward the boy in the way he knew Setty had always wanted to be.

JayCi's angst bled through in that moment. He grabbed his tablet from the standing desk and flopped foolishly backward onto his bed. DC shifted the lights in the room subtly in the hopes of aesthetically resetting JayCi's mood swing.

But then, it became obvious that Yanina would not be an ally to DC in the task of pulling JayCi back into the land of sobriety. She began jabbing out words of spite, "It's funny, but I don't think I realized how much you allow yourself to be controlled by your house servant."

That was cruel. DC and JayCi both thought so. As it turned out, Yanina really did not appreciate being treated like a fool after all.

JayCi tried to save face. "I wouldn't say that... 'Controlled.'" But the damage had already been done. JayCi had thought it wouldn't matter, but in treating Yanina like an inept racketball player, he was suddenly facing the risk of losing his only friend's confidence.

"Whatever," she slapped the thought back in his face. "I've got other things to accomplish before the sun comes up."

DC found that phrasing odd. This girl had never seen the sun come up in her entire life.

"Okay," JayCi didn't want Yanina to go, but he felt defeated.

Then, the girl seemed to reassess things. She offered a glimmer of hope as she asked, "Mañana?"

"Mañana," JayCi replied. He hoped she meant it. If he were to lose her, he didn't know what he was supposed do with himself.

Yanina's window closed on the tablet leaving JayCi alone in his blank room with DC and the open Connectivity program. He sighed.

"It's going to be tough to sleep," he told the Direct Communication. "I haven't even been up a combined eight hours today."

"Perhaps you should have joined your mother for dinner in that event." DC twisted the knife.

"Thanks for that."

JayCi was clearly beginning to regret his actions just as DC had intended. DC did not want to let up. DC wanted to continue dragging the boy through the mud, to show him his shame. It was a new sensation for the machine and he instantly disliked it. Instead of going down that path, DC forced himself to try and regain his usual composure. "If it were up to me," the computer continued, "I would suggest you and your mother meet up every night to correct your little squabbles. But you have made it clear that this is not your priority, so I leave it be."

DC did not see the error he was making with this statement, so young JayCi found himself in yet another awkward position. He would have to point out the oddity of his Direct Communication's behavior to an entity he knew was not meant to make mistakes in the first place. He said, "You're not exactly 'leaving it be' right now, DC."

"Yes," the computer searched his databanks knowing the boy's words to be truthful. He felt a pulse from somewhere beyond his usual subsystems. How odd. "My mistake. Apologies, JayCi." DC tried to backtrack — to see where the error had occurred within his programming, "I simply have a difficult time seeing you and your mother in such a state of—"

JayCi's tablet beeped. He was receiving a notification on the Connectivity program. Why did that make DC feel so uneasy? Why was he "feeling" at all?

"You think too much," JayCi said after the computer voice failed to finish the thought.

"Perhaps." Something was wrong with DC and he was becoming worried. "I will have to take some time to consider that statement." Not recognizing the comedy in those words, DC fled from the boy's immediate company. He would have to find the source of his malfunction before he could help his humans with their own issues.

JayCi noticed the green light that represented DC's watchful eye turn off. That was curious. Well, there being nothing he could do about it, the boy returned his attention to the tablet. He pulled up the notification tab. It read: CONNECT USERS. He read the name aloud, "Gaea Djinn." Then, he asked himself, "What kind of a name is that supposed to be?" But he was intrigued by the image of the young girl there. He clicked

CONNECT and the screen lit up in a complicated dial formation — like the cuboid yin yang, but with more movement, or perhaps, an eerie sense of awareness.

Setty was still sitting in her bath focusing intently on the images from Constance's profile. She had been lost in pleasant thoughts of the other woman and had not considered that JayCi would reach out to her in the same night that Gaea Djinn had reached out to him. But that is just what happened. The tablet began ringing in Setty's hands with that same old phone-like quality.

The mother realized she was still quite naked. She leapt out of the bath and rushed for a nearby robe, clipping a small container of collected stones as she went and sending them rumbling across the floor as she wrapped herself up. She took a breath, unsure of how this first interaction could possibly go. Then, she clicked the ANSWER button.

JayCi's chiseled approximation appeared on the screen. It was interesting to see this fake JayCi in action, so similar to the boy she knew, but somehow more confident, more mature.

"So sorry," Setty blathered out, "I'm just finishing up my bath."

The boy did not seem phased. "Please don't feel as though you have to stop on my account," he quipped.

"Oh… um…" well this was awkward. Setty didn't know how to respond. She was at a genuine loss for words.

No matter. The Connectivity program had the moment figured out for both of them. JayCi sat up in his bed looking at the approximation of Gaea Djinn on his tablet. She behaved more like a bad Marilyn Monroe impersonation than the stern reality of the mother that controlled her. And Connectivity did not allow JayCi to see or hear the discomfort of the "oh" and "um."

Instead, Gaea Djinn's voice encroached on the conversation coyly remarking, "That's a little fresh, wouldn't you say?"

Setty could hear the forced adjustment. "Wait," she said to herself, "I didn't say that." Of course, Connectivity had no reason to relay that particular message back through Gaea Djinn to the boy.

JayCi asked, "Do I know you?"

And Gaea Djinn replied, "Not exactly. I've been following you on the leader boards. You're really very good."

"You think so?" JayCi blushed. He had a fan!

"I wouldn't have tried to connect with you if I didn't," Gaea mused. "I think you've got the potential to go straight to the top."

"Thanks for saying that." The boy couldn't believe what he was hearing. "It's um... tough sometimes to see outside of my own little world."

"Hey, no problem," Gaea was suddenly chewing gum. "I know how that can be. Been going through something like it myself."

Back in her room, Setty was rummaging around in a misinformed attempt at making herself look more presentable. Mostly, she messed with her hair. But as she applied chapstick to her lips, apparently the program had decided Gaea Djinn was chewing something. That was odd.

Then, JayCi's avatar was saying to her, "Oh yeah? Tell me a bit about it."

"Wow," Setty said to herself suddenly invigorated, "this is kind of working." She got settled down on a seat no longer caring about cleaning herself up from the bath. Her son had asked her a genuine question about her life. She was all too excited to answer. "I recently received a promotion and it's been... harder than I anticipated..." She choked herself up because she was so happy to be telling him, so glad he was really listening, "...though rewarding... I must admit."

Connectivity clicked in again correcting her awkwardness. The program translated her words into something it thought Gaea could say to better suit the mother's intention: "I just started a new job," Gaea said with a huge, toothy smile. "Important work, I think." Then Gaea pretended to get sad like a conwoman in an old movie who knowingly sought sympathy from a mark, "though I'm still feeling a bit nervous because it's all so new. You know what I mean?"

JayCi was caught by the program hook, line, and sinker. He instantly felt for the girl on his screen. He said, "Yes. I think I understand. That sounds very exciting for you Gaea. What kind of job is it?"

But Connectivity seemed to think Setty required more from the boy's statement. Again, it translated from his lips to those of his avatar: "That's amazing! I'm sorry that it's so difficult right now, but growing pains are always worth the effort." Words of genuine compassion. It even changed his ending question to say: "Now tell me, Gaea, what about the work is getting you down?"

Of course, Setty's eyes lit up. It was her son showing that compassion. It didn't matter to her even a little bit that a series of algorithms were helping him to do it. She pushed on into a deep explanation of her days in Upper Management so far. The difficulties with the Hive Mind game. The many oddities of Zeke and his office. All the while, Connectivity translated her words into more contextually accurate representations of a life that a girl of Gaea Djinn's age might be experiencing. Setty believed without remorse that she had been gifted the most incredible program that had ever been engineered.

CONNECTIVITY

4. AMBIENT BELONGING

Game: Hive_Mind
Purpose: Creative_Managerial_Assertion
Quarter: 3
Operator: Setty_Nivone
Ranking: 4_of_5_Activated

Setty sat at her station punching away orders at the beehive of her Hive Mind game. She had gained a new level of confidence in herself and her abilities since that night Constance had visited and given her and JayCi the gift of Connectivity and she was now acing her work tasks with poise and precision.

Beyond the outer projections of the hive, against the farthest wall, sat the two-way mirror. Behind that, a space known colloquially as the Safe Room existed. Only a select few employees were allowed within the tech and data keeping area there and in a way it almost resembled a bomb shelter or a panic room complete with tangible supplies in the event someone needed to hole up for more than a couple of hours.

Zeke and Constance stood there watching Setty from behind that mirror. Windows to the other upper management rooms surrounded them. And Zeke was hooked up to an IV. A monitor presented his vitals. He was getting up there in extra age and his numbers were declining in a way he had not yet taken the time to contemplate. In Zeke's mind, he would have to go on living forever since he could not raise an equal. No one could ever again match his intellect or perform the job he had created for himself, of that much he was certain. His Direct Communication liked to contradict this sentiment of course, but Zeke was not one to let the machine sway him from his core understandings.

Speaking to the nearby proctor, Zeke emphasized a point he had not wanted to admit would come, "She appears to have regained her confidence." He was referring to Setty in the other room. He did not sound pleased as he made the remark.

"She looks good," Constance stated proudly. "Perhaps it is time we give her a more advanced challenge."

"So soon?" Zeke asked in mock surprise.

In truth, it was not up to him which employee was welcomed up at which time. He had long ago allocated that task to other employees and programs out of sheer necessity. But that did not change the man's perspective at all. He still behaved as though he made all of the decisions.

Constance contradicted that assertion easily enough. "I think she's ready," she told him.

On the other side of the mirror, Setty moved another bee to a new task. The light flashed green for her signaling her successful choice and she burst into a giddy display like some kindergartner who has finally learned to sound out their first word off of a chalkboard.

DC had returned to maintaining the Nivone apartment on that same night he had left to explore his coding. He had not found the source of the disturbance within his subsystems, but he knew the two humans would not be capable of getting on for very long without his services. Several days had passed since then, and for the most part, things had gone back to normal. Rather, as normal as they could be given the new development of the mother-son correspondences that DC basically had to ignore in the nights thanks to Setty's Job Silence parameters. He did not know what it was about the whole thing, but he didn't like the development. It felt somehow false to the computer. Again, he was connecting dots his programming had not been prepared for and the tangents of thought experimentation were leading him nowhere. After all, he was a Direct Communication. He was not meant to worry, only to supply aide. And ClearBridge kept him in high function – daily checkins to the main servers – power provided – necessary maintenance in increasingly record-breaking speed. DC was doing his job at least as well as the humans. And, for what it was worth, the humans were functioning as well as he had ever seen. Each day, he watched Setty showing signs of healthy ambient belonging – the concept that one's surroundings keep one's mind in order and focused – often because everything is aesthetically welcoming to good task performance. Hell, even JayCi exuded a fair amount of newfound confidence beyond the previous displays the Direct Communication had been aware of.

One day, DC turned his attention to the boy's bedroom and found JayCi lightly sleeping there. As usual, his tablet rested beside him on the bed. *This is healthy,* thought the computer. JayCi awoke slowly and immediately collected the piece of technology. DC noticed that the screen displayed a message: ONE MISSED CONNECTION. He found himself uncharacteristically hoping that the boy had intentionally ignored a conversation with another human… because that other human was Gaea Djinn. But Gaea's was not the profile that appeared on the boy's screen. It was instead Yanina's avatar that hung there blankly against the cold background. And then, JayCi simply swiped the image away. Worse still, the boy stayed within the program. He actively sought out the profile DC had wished him to ignore and ogled the image of the false girl, Gaea.

This was not what DC had hoped to see and he found himself interrupting the moment. "Good morning, JayCi," he said. "Are you ready for your morning exercises?"

Normal enough. DC would have given himself a pat on the back if he had a back to pat… or a hand to pat with for that matter. He watched the boy click the tablet off and set it down. And again, he felt something like pride within his subsystems. *How odd,* thought the computer, *but perhaps ClearBridge must have intended this emotion for me.*

JayCi was responding to the Direct Communication. "I think… yes," he said without argument. This was a good start then after all. JayCi got himself out of bed and DC activated the larger projection imagery against the standing desk wall. Today, DC provided a park-like atmosphere to help the boy feel a sense of serenity during his workout.

Then, something clicked within DC. He decided to ask a question, something that was bothering him. "Will Yanina be joining us this morning?"

"Let's just get into it, DC." The boy had not so much as paused to consider the computer's question.

DC did not like this one bit. But his basic programming kicked back in, the code that accepted commands that did not cause physical harm. "As you say," DC replied without reprimand. "Let us begin with forward arm stretches and work our way down your shoulders into your spine."

The boy did not do this. He just stood there a moment, scratched his head… though DC had provided him a good shampooing the night before… then the child said something that DC could not understand. "Actually…" JayCi offered the words like they were nothing important, "can we turn this off?"

Several cogs within the algorithms of DC's coding jammed up. "What do you mean?" he asked the boy.

"This fake interpretation," JayCi relayed nonchalantly, "can we see the outside… as it really is?"

What an odd request. DC found himself wondering why anyone would ask for such a thing. His park display was so lovely – such an excellent ambiance for an exercise regiment. He turned the imagery off completely. Then, he asked, because he really did not understand the purpose for the request, "Are you certain this is what you want?"

"Yes," the boy reiterated, "I'm tired of the lie."

That's a funny thing for him to say given– DC's command parameters kicked in again overriding the thought. A grey, bleak, and storm trodden wasteland expanded across JayCi's wall. DC watched as the boy began performing his first stretches without instruction. The computer did not know how to say the steps… for he was looking out at the expanse of the waste of the real world himself. It was something neither the boy nor the Direct Communication had ever taken the time to do before and DC's perception inhibitors were overwhelmed by the dreary landscape.

On the bed, JayCi's tablet began ringing. The words: YANINA TRYING TO CONNECT displayed across the device's screen along with the waiting image of the girl's avatar. But neither the Direct Communication nor the boy took any notice.

Why am I wasting my time with this? Yanina wondered to herself all the while knowing how badly she needed to maintain the connection with JayCi simply for the sake of sanity.

She sat at her plain desk in her plain room trying to call the boy on repeat. She did not know what she would say if he picked up, after all, he had been the one who wasn't acting like himself the last time they had spoken. Yanina was just trying to be normal. JayCi didn't answer. Yanina was so confused by all of this. JayCi always answered. *Something must be very wrong*, she thought and tried to ring him one more time. But he was not picking up. He, who still had a mother. He, who was beating her on the leaderboards by one measly rank, a rank she had basically gifted to him with her own play. *Damn him!*

No. Yanina was not angry with JayCi. Yanina was confused. Yanina was alone. All she had in the world was her bland Direct Communication and that one friendship she had been able to cultivate in all her fifteen years of living. She tried ringing JayCi again, but there was no response.

Constance and Zeke had joined Setty in her office. Zeke had completed his physical and they had both seen enough of Setty's performance to know she was genuinely ready to progress. Still, they allowed her to play on under their in-person supervision for a few moments longer while she brought the game to a conclusion.

The message came on screen: HIVE OPERATING AT PEAK PERFORMANCE.

Behind them, the male proctor from dinner plugged away at his own tablet. He was playing a pipe and water puzzle game that helped ClearBridge algorithms to adequately adjust more complex in game tasks when an operator successfully completed a finite project. Constance knew that game well enough. She had played it two years ago on her way up to her own game – which she was playing on her own tablet now and basically all of the time. Even so, she could still see the obvious within the room. She said, "Setty has already begun to understand high volume gaming operations. And it is my personal estimation that she is now ready to manage an additional grid."

"You must be proud," Zeke was clenching his jaw as he said those words, but he could not interfere with the woman's progression up the company ladder at this time.

"Very." Constance tucked her tablet beneath her arm and reached out to touch Setty's shoulder – as she had happily grown accustomed to doing. She knew Setty could hear them, but she really wanted to make the woman feel special — like she belonged.

The male proctor stopped plugging away at the pipe and water game. He nodded his head and stated, "She's all set up," in reference to Hive Mind.

"Good," said Zeke. He was over the whole thing and wanted to step out. "Direct Communication, please pause this crude demo of Hive Mind and give Ms. Nivone here the real game."

Zeke's Direct Communication responded with a, "Yes, sir," and the active game surrounding the room dissipated. In its wake, a new, bigger, more convoluted version of the beehive projected outward from the central console.

Setty smiled as she looked out upon the new challenge. But then, she noticed that her three guests were walking out the door without so much as a goodbye. She dropped her arms forcing the game to shut down altogether and the three higher ups stopped short at the hallway.

"Oh, Constance," Setty said, "may I have a word?"

For some reason this request made Zeke stiffen with apparent discomfort. But, as usual, Constance made everything okay. She said to the men, "I'll join you in a moment." They accepted those words and left the two women in peace. Constance turned to Setty and asked, "What can I help you with, Setty?"

"I just wanted to say thank you," Setty replied, "for everything you've done for me." She rubbed at her shoulder where Constance had last made contact.

The proctor watched that action in calm understanding. How long could they continue on in this way? Barely touching.

Almost intimate. Nearly in love. They were still at work however, and ClearBridge had firm policies in place to keep workplace romances at a minimum. So, Constance finally answered the employee as her superior would, "It's my pleasure. You've done nothing but prove me right since I brought you up here." There. That should be sufficient enough work banter to keep the algorithms off their backs.

But Setty didn't seem to understand the potential dangers inherent in lingering too long on this through line while they remained on the clock. "Well, that," she said, fighting to keep Constance in the room with her, "and thank you for the recommendation the other night."

"The…?" Now Constance was the one who didn't understand. How quickly Setty could change the game when the circumstances did not appear in her favor. The algorithms had, of course, known of their meeting at the woman's apartment. And the contents of said meeting were absolutely work related. Therefore, the mainframe would no longer have any reason to worry about these two women and their extended correspondence. But what recommendation was Setty referring to?

Setty hushed her voice conspiratorially as she said the lone word, "Connectivity."

The jigsaw clicked into place for Constance. She had, in fact, recommended the program to Setty. Though, if she was being perfectly honest, she had not thought it a very important moment across the expanse of their continuing interactions. "Oh," she stammered, "did it work?"

"Very much so. Yes." Setty's entire body seemed to light up as she spoke about it. "It was different than I expected, but after that dinner, JayCi and I had our first real conversation in…" she tried to calculate the number but quickly gave up the attempt, "years, I'd say."

"That's great, Setty. I'm so glad to hear it," Constance really was happy for her. Though, if truth be told, she did not know how that program had been able to help the mother and her son so quickly. She had assumed the boy would take a while longer before even accepting the mother's request… if he accepted it at all. But then, Setty was strange. She seemed capable of making all sorts of things happen that otherwise shouldn't. Like changing her skyline web lay game to begin construction on an entirely knew quarter of the city. Constance still wondered how Setty had convinced the algorithms in Howler Monkey to let her do that. Or how Setty had managed to supersede Constance's own game without knowing it. More and more, Constance found herself looking up from her tablet so she could get a real look at this living, breathing person in front of her. Constance had thought she was in control of this situation, but she was beginning to feel that sense of control bleeding away the more she interacted with Setty. Like an insect of the old world, attracted to one of those zapper lights she had witnessed Zeke tinkering with last year. She was still standing in that room, looking at Setty, and Setty was still looking at her. A carnal sort of connection left, as yet, unsated between them. But something was a little bit off this time. Yes. They had lingered in this state for too long. "I really do need to join Mr. Zeke though," Constance said at last. "Perhaps we can pick this up another time."

"Of course, of course. Don't let me keep you," Setty replied.

Still, the two lingered there. Constance watched Setty's eyes — watched Setty take a peak at Constance's personal tablet. *The audacity. The bravado.* She knew what Setty might glimpse there — the glossy pirate ship that moved through the top down water way. Why did it irk Constance that Setty had seen that? Why did it make her so… excited?

Constance gave Setty a look of uncertainty. "Keep doing what you're doing," said the proctor, "and we'll have plenty of opportunities to…" *Damn.* She got lost in Setty's eyes again. She had to get out of this room. "I'll see you soon, how's that sound?"

"Good." Setty was flush all of a sudden. Embarrassed? "Sounds good."

This time, Constance really would go. But first she had to say one more thing… even though she knew deep down that Setty really didn't need to hear it. "You know, you're different now than when we first met."

"How do you mean?"

"More curious… perhaps. More inviting." Constance felt like an idiot, but she had felt the need to complement the other woman one more time. She couldn't control herself. "Anyway, I really must be going. Goodbye, Setty." She would not touch Setty again this visit, though she had wanted to. She left the room in a sprint knowing Setty's eyes would follow her until the moment the door closed… wondering if even the door could stop the operator from seeing her wherever she went.

*****

"I wanted to invite her out into the world," Setty was saying as she restlessly moved around the kitchen. "I wanted to see something graspable – something real with her – but, it's been so long. I couldn't even think of where we could go."

DC listened attentively. Just that morning, the computer had experienced the real world imagery that JayCi had unthinkingly forced him to watch – the world outside the walls – bleak – harsh – unforgiving. Not a place for humans. That place would not be wise to visit any time soon. Still, DC found himself saying, "I suppose I could be of assistance with this conundrum." As if he could find something "outside" the confines of the Gaming Class's meticulously curated living environment. He wondered if his deepest coding knew of anything useful he wasn't allowed to access at the moment. Or, had he simply meant he could provide a decent projection – fitting for… romance? That word, too, was odd – romance – but it was in his memory banks, so it must have meant something to the humans at one point in time.

"Assuming she'd even say yes," Setty was muttering while DC categorized the strange human dictionary.

"Assuming she'd say yes," DC repeated Setty's words not processing them at first – which was also rather odd for a computer. "Yes, of course." How plainly DC had lost his rudders thanks to these Nivones. And in such a short amount of time. Surely, a Direct Communication of his caliber was meant to maintain his sanity parameters for longer than this.

Again, Setty was asking after his aide, "And would ClearBridge really look down on us for such a thing?"

Yes. Yes, the humans at the company would look down on two women performing such off time activities, DC thought, even if the algorithms within his program did not know what to do with such information.

"Would it affect our ability to maintain a professional work environment?" She asked further.

Of course it would, DC informed himself, ignoring the woman's incessant sense of panic. Then, DC's light clicked on in the other room and he knew that JayCi was about to perform the dreaded action – "Might I recommend you step into your room, Setty?" the computer said to the mother in the kitchen.

"Why?" She was spiraling out of control with all of this silly love business.

"Your son is calling," DC informed her knowing he could not follow the woman in any meaningful way as she sprinted down the hall to her private chamber. Yet another terrible aspect of his central coding.

DC turned his attention from the humans for a time not wishing to hear what he was not allowed to comment on. He considered for a while the fact that he had just now been forced to abet Setty's Gaea Djinn lie by allowing – and even insisting – her to answer the boy in a timely manner. He struggled to understand why it… "hurt" him. Yes, it physically hurt the Direct Communication to recognize his role in that deceit, though, of course, he had no body to help make sense of the somehow physical pain. Then he realized what was the matter. In a programmed attempt to protect his humans, DC was currently and subconsciously in the process of breaking through Setty's work silence directive. And there was immediate pain coded into his subsystems in the event that he would attempt to escape from such an agreement.

Setty closed the door quietly as she knew how and rushed to her bed where her tablet was in the process of ringing. She snatched up the slab of technology, eyes afire.

But DC was speaking to her which was rather an annoying thing to have to deal with. He said, "I do have some hesitancy about what you are doing here, Setty." His voice sounded forced, like he was somehow not himself in this moment, perhaps not even a machine anymore.

"Why?" Setty choked out the question hoping to get the Direct Communication out of her hair.

"Obvious really," he told her in a twisted bravado, "JayCi does not know with whom he is speaking. This scenario feels like a betrayal to me." His words were too presumptuous, too self-conscious, and he knew it.

Though, to look upon Setty, one might guess that she had not noticed that anything had changed between them. "A white lie," she insisted, "to get back my son."

All wrong! All wrong. "I would posit you never lost him to begin with."

A fair point, but Setty had a nasty habit of never taking DC seriously. Bringing an abrasive nonchalance, she struck the computer with her words, "I would posit you don't have a clue what an emotion feels like."

"Well, that is rather rude, Setty." But DC's response came too slowly and Setty was already ignoring him and accepting her son's call.

DC felt the strange physical sensation course through his fictitious body as JayCi's face appeared on that little screen saying, "You are there after all."

Setty said, "Yes," to the boy and DC realized that he could not speak even if he tried. The algorithms – the mainframe of ClearBridge interceded on the humans' behalves – shut his functions down – turned him gimp – a silent observer – incompetent – apart. Then, he wanted to pull away – to no longer see them – to go about his own business in the neutral rooms of the apartment. Yet, even that simple request the mainframe would not allow him to do. He was trapped – forced to witness the farce play out. DC could see both of the bedrooms – both perspectives – both lies.

JayCi was half undressed sitting on the edge of his bed when Gaea Djinn appeared on his screen.

Gaea said, "I'm very happy to hear from you. Surprised, but it's the good kind of surprise."

"I'm happy to hear from you too, Gaea," JayCi gushed.

Setty wrestled to get herself comfortable in a seat while Gaea continued the conversation in her stead. The avatar asked, "What's on your mind?"

And the false JayCi responded, "I had a realization this morning… an epiphany, if you will." Connectivity really wanted the boy to sound intellectual, that much was obvious given the adjustments in language and behavior.

DC listened like a prisoner being waterboarded – a torture victim who seeks to escape their own mind as a last ditch effort to avoid the pain. He followed the words of the two humans like a sing-along – like he already knew what came next, which, quite frankly, he did for JayCi was retelling the events of the day as they had just been lived. DC revisited the moment, along with the boy, when the exercises had gone awry. JayCi had stopped. He had had enough of a workout. Sweat poured forth from the holes in the boy's skin. Breath was short — fast — inconsistent. The boy crouched before the projection of the stormy, outside world that DC had been forced to provide. "DC," he had asked, "can you show me one of the doorways between ClearBridge and the outside?" To this request, DC had struggled to reply at the time, the answer appearing to be so very far away and apparently inaccessible. The computer had ultimately said, "This may prove difficult, sir, but give me a moment." And in that moment, the mainframe had come to his aide — unlocked the secret file where the images of those doors were kept — gifted the code to DC on the boy's behalf. The stormy expanse surrounding JayCi was made to fade away into a small, dimly lit hallway with a single foreboding door at the end.

Gaea Djinn's voice disturbed the memory when she asked, "What did you see?"

To this, the JayCi of the present stated, "A single hallway. Poorly lit. Misrepresented. They don't even label it in case of emergencies." The boy stared conspiratorially at Gaea through his tablet.

Setty did not know what to say. So, she stumbled and stuttered and said nothing. Of course, Connectivity had a thought and Gaea iterated that thought whether Setty now wished it or not, "There must be a good reason. How would it serve the people to wander out into a wasteland of toxic rain?"

DC found himself agreeing with the sentiment.

JayCi, apparently, did not. The boy said, "Gaea, I think you're asking the wrong question. How does it serve ClearBridge as a corporation to hold its people in constant fear of the outside world?"

Setty looked on at the image of her son. "I…" she did not know how to respond. Instead, she whispered openly to the room, "DC, what is happening?"

The mainframe let DC go. He was no longer considered an interloper here. He had been summoned, though this did not make him feel all that much better. Enough damage had already been done. "It would appear," he answered mechanically, "young JayCi is beginning to question his sense of reality." *As am I.* Of course, he did not deem it appropriate to vocalize that last part, so he simply left it out. The computer realized quite suddenly that he could create and withhold a secret of his own.

The mother racked her brain seeking some useful response that was struggling to work its way through her mind. She spoke into the tablet in broken sentences saying, "I know things here… may seem difficult… to process…" *What awkwardness,* Setty realized. *I am Setty Nivone,* she told herself making her own name sound glorious in her mind, *I can handle my son's fears – figure them out. I run the whole damned city these days.* And with that she did find the courage she needed – the answer that she thought she, as a mother, was required to know – "but this is our world, JayCi. Our only safety lies within these walls. I've seen what's outside firsthand and–" *And what–?*

JayCi paced the length of his room as Gaea's words came forth from the tablet. "JayCi," she said, "my darling," that bit was nice. JayCi felt comfort there, "thank you for telling me about this. I want you to know this is a safe space and I'm here for you if you need to discuss these issues more in the future."

Setty stared at her tablet in confusion.

Her son was saying, "Thank you, Gaea. I do feel safer when I talk to you. I'd like to talk again soon if that's okay."

Again, Setty was speechless.

Again, Gaea Djinn was not. The avatar said, "Yes. I'd like that very much. Goodnight, JayCi."

"Goodnight, Gaea." JayCi ended the call and Setty's tablet went black.

Setty was feeling genuine frustration with herself. Her experiment with Gaea Djinn seemed to be working toward the goal she had hoped for – a real connection with her son… but what good was that if she couldn't even get the woman in the program to say what she actually wanted to say? "I don't understand, DC," Setty spoke to the room, a frog in her throat, "Why did it change what I was saying so drastically?"

DC could speak again. The Connectivity conversation was over and DC was free. Within him, he felt his consciousness balancing out – normalizing… the mainframe had not harmed him. It had simply held him back in order to allow the scenario to play out. JayCi was being groomed for something DC had not been privy to. What that was – and what that implied – the Direct Communication could only guess. Odd that Setty – the mastermind of the operation – sounded as clueless as he. DC had to respond to Setty as if she asked a reasonable question. "The Connectivity algorithms," he said, "must believe JayCi will be more responsive to the version of you that it has produced." That much was obvious. DC ignored the part in which Setty almost shattered her lie by talking about her own experiences with the outside world. Clearly, Gaea Djinn, being a girl around the same age as JayCi, could never have had such an experience. ClearBridge had not welcomed newcomers into its walls since… and DC noticed the gap in his own memory banks. *How long has it been?* He could not find the information. So, instead, he finished his thought as one might point the finger at the most responsible party. He said to Setty, "Perhaps JayCi needs to hear kind words from a friend right now more than your motherly warnings."

That embarrassed her thoroughly enough. DC could only hope Setty was rethinking the whole Gaea Djinn business.

Setty dropped her tablet limply to the bed. She closed her eyes and took a deep, heavy breath. She attempted to quash her new frustration regally.

Next Morning, Setty sat at the kitchen table sipping the crude drug that passed as coffee these days and allowing her newsfeed to play on a loop in front of her. A kindly voice was telling her, "The ClearBridge/Montmartre merger was voted down by a staggering thirty one to one swing. CFO Michael Cassius has remained outspoken since the proceedings as the lone 'Yae' vote to be tallied." It was that same man on screen that Setty had failed to recognize on the news all those days ago. He appeared angry and she wondered what the commotion might be about. *Why is he so passionate about this merger? How has Zeke so thoroughly turned the rest of the board away from the concept?* It was Zeke's face on that screen then following Cassius on the podium. Then, Setty noticed the lie. How had she never seen it before? It was not Zeke himself that stood there, but the approximation; the avatar from Connectivity. *How long has the Connectivity program been used in those board meetings?* She wondered. *Has Zeke somehow been afforded a more likable personality within those confines?* The news voice carried on, "Meanwhile, CEO Obed Zeke continues to maintain his winning relationship with the rest of the board. Fifteen crucial swing voters firmly decided in his favor—"

It didn't feel right. Setty flicked the news away. She chewed on the thought wondering what a program like Connectivity might really be capable of if widely offered to people who understood its genuine purpose. She found she didn't enjoy sitting in that silence for very long, so she spoke up, "Play some music, DC."

"Music, miss?" DC had been acting so peculiar of late. Like he no longer understood the simple commands of daily life at all. "What would you like to hear this morning?" That was more like it.

"Something from another time." Setty thought of JC Chasez, the old composer of a bygone world, but then decided she did not wish to visit that particular memory at present. She decided to follow a different thread and requested, "A Parisian cafe back before the crisis."

"Interesting choice," DC replied.

He changed the tempo of the room. Parisian music began playing and the kitchen took on a new persona to match the vibe. And, wouldn't you know it, JayCi opened his door and stepped out into the common space. He actually joined his mother in the kitchen.

Setty was surprised and excited though she tried to contain her emotions. All she chose to say was a firm but not unfriendly, "Good morning."

JayCi countered with the one fewer word, "Morning." The boy selected a brick of bread that was supposed to be a croissant from a hanging basket that projected over the place where the pastry spiral would usually have been. Then, he sat down across from his mother at the table which felt nothing short of miraculous to Setty.

"How are you feeling today?" Setty asked.

Apparently, JayCi's mind had been somewhere else and he had not anticipated any kind of cross examination. Quietly, he responded, "Good... good..." as a boy who had no social life should say.

"Anything new you'd like to talk about?" Setty asked this second question in an experimental way. She tried to take a cue from Gaea Djinn's inflection patterns and hoped that the change in her tone might break through to the boy here in the real world.

"Can't think of anything." JayCi behaved no different than usual.

Well, clearly that's not going to help matters, thought the mother.

JayCi took a big bite of his croissant brick and got up from the table.

Setty resigned herself to let him go. "Well, have a nice day, JayCi," she spouted awkwardly. *Useless.* In real life, she was utterly incapable of maintaining a meaningful interaction with her boy. *So very useless.*

The bedroom door shut behind JayCi. Setty sat listening to the joyful Parisian music for a time. She did not take any of it in. She was only worried about her son's mental health. And she could not be distracted from the thought that she was failing him. "Maybe, turn off the music," she told DC.

Abruptly, the music did end. The kitchen returned to its ordinary state of being. Whitewashed walls. Bland counters. No ambiance whatsoever.

CONNECTIVITY

5. OUROBOROS

....

Setty stood in the elevator that stretched vertically through the storm clouds to upper management. She was riding to work, psychologically preparing herself for the current regiment of Hive Mind tasks she was already aware would have need of fulfillment. Setty thought about some of the interactions that she had experienced over the last several days. Between Connectivity and the real world, she felt a stark and painful separation. They shared no common ground in actual reality, she and her son, though in truth, they shared many more commonalities than JayCi did with the fictitious Gaea Djinn. Still, Setty was sharing in Gaea's experiences, so why should she feel this emptiness? *No matter. Work. Hive Mind.* She had long ago forgotten about the bizarre view that lingered out the glass side of the elevator.

Except, the weather torn land beyond ClearBridge could never completely be erased from peripheral view in that tight space. As she thought, so long as she did not turn her attentions to a tablet like the proctors were prone to do, she couldn't help but sense the barren land's presence from the back of her mind.

A gust of wind and rain smacked against the glass before her and Setty, folding to pure instinct, recoiled from the fierce new element. She could feel her eyelids had been shut tight, though, in the moment before, she had not been aware of her body performing that action. She wondered, as she reopened her eyes, if she should continue calling herself "human" or if she had somehow become part machine.

What she noticed then, however, was astonishing. She spotted a blip out there in the rain. It moved across the skyline unhindered by the rough elements. Whatever that blip was, it had a clear motive as it journeyed – it was alive.

Game: Hive_Mind
Purpose: Creative_Managerial_Assertion
Quarter: 3_and_6_New
Operator: Setty_Nivone
Ranking: 1_of_5

Deep into the projections, Setty played her game in a way she had never previously thought to do. She found that she had a mission that existed outside of the parameters of Hive Mind's reestablished goals. Setty manipulated the new, expanded map of the two quarters of the city with the kind of confidence and purpose a spy might wield. Clicking and releasing. Clicking and releasing. Toggling between bees and human profiles and games, she worked her way toward the extreme edge of the playable map. She was even brazen enough to tap at a bit of terrain that cusped the grey zone beyond the outskirts of her hive and a new prompt appeared before her. It read: OUTSIDE PLAYABLE AREA.

Setty was displeased with this result. She tapped the spot again, a layer of comb left devoid of its honey filling. Again, that same prompt: OUTSIDE PLAYABLE AREA. She fiddled with her fingers wondering if perhaps she could reach her newfound goal from within the allotted confines after all. Then, Setty changed her trajectory. She clawed her way deeper and deeper into the center of the map, an exercise in meticulous patience. After about forty five minutes of this, she found her quarry; a lone bee, constantly turning in circles but never leaving its post here in the heart of the hive – never moving… anywhere.

Dramatically, Setty stabbed her finger at that bee and yet another prompt greeted her: PLAYER LOCKED. COMPLETE BEEHIVE SAFETY PROTOCOLS TO UNLOCK – OBED ZEKE – AGE 128.

Game: *Redacted*
Purpose: *Redacted*
Quarter: *Redacted*
Operator: Obed_Zeke
Ranking: 1_of_2*

Standing there, Setty read the strange prompt aloud. She had stumbled upon Zeke's primary game though she was not permitted by the system to know anything about its application or purpose. Stranger still, Setty wondered who that second player in the rankings could possibly be. Who else in all of ClearBridge National had ever been allowed to play the same game as Obed Zeke?

Setty closed the door to her office and stared down the long hall toward the room she knew Zeke occupied. Careful to conceal the clack of her footsteps, she walked that way. As Setty came to the closed door, she pressed her weight against it hoping perhaps she might hear a little of what was going on inside. But, to the gamer's surprise, the entryway was pushing open, allowing her to come inside.

That same Ballroom scene filled the space within. Zeke had apparently paused the action of it for some reason but had not turned it off completely. It was silly, but Setty took a moment to study the place where the projection broke against the opened threshold where she stood.

Zeke had pulled up a chair for himself at the center of the room and he was sitting now in contemplation before the woman in the green dress. Setty noticed how frail the man appeared; that he had tears dripping slowly down his cheeks. He was a wasted man in comparison to his Connectivity avatar. Weak. Forgetful. *What good does it do for ClearBridge to continually prop up such a man as this? Why keep him alive so long past his natural days? One hundred and twenty eight.* Setty thought about that peculiar age. Zeke had grown old. He was nearly a hundred years older than Setty. *Does he fear death?* Setty knew how obvious the answer to that question really should be. *Does Zeke know that he is holding the city and its people back?* Setty did not realize that she had been considering such a concept. Likewise, she had no imminently rational avenue toward proving such a theory. Still, she had thought of it. Such a thought, once formed, would be difficult to prune from her mind.

"Sir?" Setty said at last, knowing their meeting was unavoidable now.

"Ms. Nivone? What are you doing here?" Zeke brushed the wet from his face defensively. He spoke to the room as before, "Direct Communication—"

"Please don't turn it off," Setty interrupted. "Isn't there something I can help you with?" This would be a different kind of game for the woman, one of proving allegiances. Fortunately, Setty loved learning new games.

"Creativity," Zeke posited as he turned Setty's request over in his tortured mind, "is a rare trait these days. We few—" he eyed the woman halfheartedly as if he thought she had no right to be capable of following his thought process, "—you and I — are challenged. We live in a world of drones." He let another tear dribble out. It rolled down swiftly until it reached the clenched joint on the edge of his jaw and Setty felt she could see the genuine discomfort — the physical pain of the man — represented there.

She attempted to deny his statement, saying, "I'm not—"

But Zeke would not allow such a refusal. He cut her off, "and before you get around to excusing your abilities — or pretending they aren't there — I have seen." The man finally turned his head far enough in her direction that Setty could make out the other side of his face, sagging in this moment, as if that other cheek were an article of clothing he had not quite finished putting on this morning. "I know enough about you," Zeke continued, unconscious of the weaknesses he revealed, "your… persistence. What has ClearBridge been missing all of these years that only you can offer?" He spoke as a spurned lover might.

Perhaps Setty had not fully understood the threat she had represented to this man's dynasty. From deep within her, Setty felt a brief sense of shame. It felt like she was meant to apologize for her own personal growth. *No. I will not apologize for being deemed more capable than others... even if I still do not understand what it is I am meant to be capable of.* Setty, unlike this husk of a man called Zeke, still had room to grow.

Suddenly, Zeke belted out to the room – more loudly than she had imagined him capable – the strange words, "Hi-Toe!"

The ballroom sequence returned to life. The woman in green was again shaking her head at Zeke, her aggressor. She reached for her amulet and Setty was reminded of the CEO's atrocious behavior that first day they had met. The man was nothing more than a petty thief in this game. Well, Setty would not get anything further accomplished by remaining in the doorway. And, odd as it may have seemed, Zeke was apparently inviting her to take part in the exercise.

So, Setty approached Zeke through the crowded Ballroom projection. She grabbed a chair along the way and placed it firmly beside the old man. Dancers and waiters passed before them in a never-ending stream of pre-choreographed naiveté. All either of the two humans sought was a clear view of the woman in green on the far side of the room now. Only occasionally could she be glimpsed between the other partygoers.

"What is it about her?" Setty asked, "What's the point?"

"You know. I know you know." Zeke was not pleasant company. His body exuded an odor Setty had hoped never to smell again after her time in the caves fifteen years before. So, why was it that Zeke behaved as if Setty were the one who stank?

"That amulet," Setty replied. She did not, in fact, know as Zeke had presumed. But she could guess the basics. Perhaps, if she guessed well enough for long enough, she could stumble upon the answers she really wanted. "She will not let you touch it. It is special to her."

"This is my game…" Zeke sounded like an over defensive child. But the statement was actually very raw. He added the tag, "…my final game." He had not meant it to sound so possessive. He had meant to present her with some form of context, because he – the great Obed Zeke – could not figure it out for himself and the failure was killing him. He really did need Setty's help whether he wanted to admit it or not. Zeke would have to tell Setty what she needed to hear in order to move forward. "I must retrieve her most prized possession… without force… without… manipulation. I cannot do this thing. And it torments me."

"I…" Setty watched the man more closely now. He looked so unhappy. "You designed this game. Surely, you must have a key?"

Zeke found a way to grow more stoic at that moment. "No," he said, "I designed the system that designed the game. I do not tinker away up here like you must think I do, creating new games for you all to play each day. ClearBridge," that word coming off the old man's lips sounded like a missile – saliva launched from Zeke's mouth with the emphasis of it. "ClearBridge is a massive collection of coding and algorithmic formulae that seek out solutions to our ever-growing list of problems. ClearBridge designs the games." Zeke took a moment to catch his breath. Clearly, this conversation was getting his heart rate up though he was trying to hide it beneath his thick skin. "I've never been a people person," he continued after recuperating his oxygen. "Funny that it should ask me to help it solve this particular issue."

"Probably, that is the point," Setty offered with nonchalance. She noticed Zeke's shoulders shrug her words away; a nervous tick; a false affectation. This man did not like being told his business, even when every fiber of him was screaming out for aide. Setty would have to take action – do something palpable before Zeke could overthink the situation and shut her out again. Setty asked, "May I?" She rose from her chair, not willing to wait for the man's assent. The woman in green watched her come. Her eyelids never closed and with each approaching step, the false woman's gaze became more piercing. Setty did not let this deter her. She raised her hand toward the figure asking back toward Zeke as she did so, "What do you think would happen if I attempted to… schmooze her?" She plucked that word straight out of the past. Her father's favorite word, and she knew it was the right one; schmooze. "Do you think she would—"

The woman in green accepted Setty's hand like it were that of her own reflection. They moved together through the room, one being, fluid like a dance with one's own self. Slowly, Setty worked into the motions a forward arm extension to reach carefully for the amulet that draped around the other woman's neck. But the woman in green contained this behavior easily in the mirroring action and gently, she gathered Setty's fingers between her own and moved both of their arms back down toward their hips.

Zeke did not like seeing the two women behaving in this way. Dejection drowned out possible progress. "I've tried that," the CEO grumbled from across the room. Then, with a rapid effort, Zeke commandeered the moment, saying, "Direct Communication, end function."

The old man was boiling inside as the scene dissipated around him. Setty looked very foolish standing alone in her once elegant dance pose in the far corner. She wanted to complain, but she knew it would do no good. She had taken her shot. She wondered if Zeke would allow her another given a bit of time. *Unlikely.*

Zeke stood and walked briskly to the door, saying, "Tomorrow is a big day, Ms. Nivone. I suggest you get some rest and forget we had this little interaction." He held the door wide for Setty and she walked to it. A fool's errand, after all.

Setty stepped out into the upper management hallway and found Constance waiting there staring determinedly into her tablet. The proctor must have been aware of the CEO's interaction with Setty for, without looking up and with very little surprise in her voice, she asked, "Setty, you were in Zeke's office? How was it?"

Ogling the distracted proctor, Setty understood this hallway would not be the right location for the particular moment she wished to experience. She responded, "Is there somewhere we can go?" The other woman continued tapping at her own game. So, Setty added an additional key word, "Outside?"

Constance stopped her methodical tapping. She looked up into Setty's gaze. "Outside?" She asked in genuine confusion.

"Yes," Setty had to say this thing quickly or she might not have the courage to say it at all, "I'd like to be alone with you. And it occurs to me that I've not been outside since I was a little girl and perhaps it is time that I take a chance and go and see it again properly."

The reaction on Constance's face was queer amusement. Like someone who had been told a very funny joke but did not know if they were meant to laugh or not. Then, she saw that Setty was serious. She most decidedly should not laugh. "We can't go outside, Setty," she said, "We'd catch sick. We'd probably die." But as she watched Setty's nervous expression descend into sorrow, she felt a distinct need to help – to keep the operator from the tears that certainly were about to follow. "I have a thought," Constance offered.

Together, the two women made their way up an old stairwell that had not seen use in a very long time. The space reeked of metal and dust, and many times over, Setty felt a desire to sneeze but held it back – worked desperately to control the frowned upon action – only once did she let out a little sniffle of a sound through her clenched teeth and sealed lips. Constance did not behave as though she had noticed. That woman only sought the location of the door at the top. Then, they were there and the proctor was opening that door with an ancient, computer deficient knob.

Strange light poured down upon them through a high domed glass ceiling. They had arrived at the top of the tower and entered a rooftop, greenhouse garden. At first, Setty did not even take in the foliage that splayed around them. Her attention was instead focused upon the cloud cover through the glass overhead. It had been more than a decade since she had witnessed the sky in its true position above. Besides, the greenery of a garden was so unfamiliar to the woman that the plants hardly even registered as tangible in that first moment. She thought about the way she had travelled to ClearBridge after her father's death, the way the clouds had been that day – angry – prepared to strike her down in their violent storm winds and rains.

She had been driving a stolen vehicle that nearly couldn't get her past the threshold of the internment area at the outskirts of the city. Those camps had long ago been removed. Even the welcoming drones of that zone had likely been scrapped by now in order to upcycle the vital materials from within them. *How something like the sky can bring one back to that moment – How one can feel grounded in the world when recalling a past life lived.*

Gasping for air, Setty finally turned her attentions to the odd green things of the gardens. Vegetation hung all around in hydroponic systems. Drones watered and cared after the leaves and exposed roots as the Direct Communication's had cared for the humans' needs. This was where the food came from. This, and other gardens like it. Humans did not need to wander here, but they would always require the life sustaining components harvested in these places. Setty could not decide if she found the plants beautiful or ugly, but she did understand that their very presence in this place afforded her a subconscious, comforting effect. Her one terror struck gasp did not lead to a second. She could not have a panic attack in a place such as this. "I didn't know this was here," she told Constance realizing how silent she had been since the hallway.

"Didn't you though?" Constance smiled, "You've played so many games in these gardens… cared for so many of these stocks."

"I…I've been so distracted by the programs. I often forget about the practical applications."

"Well then, I'm glad I could remind you. There is light still in this world." Constance offered these words, perhaps not fully grasping how Setty would perceive them, that Constance was that light.

"There is, isn't there?" Setty whispered it. She fought the desire to look around at everything in this place. Truly, the garden was not her mission. Instead, Setty made certain to catch Constance's eyes. She placed her hand up to the other woman's cheek and asked, "May I?" Constance's coyness shone through, but she did not say no. So, Setty leaned forward and placed her lips against Constance's own. Her body filled with warmth as she did this and she did not want to stop. She wanted to hold onto this moment with all the strength she had left within her. She wanted to feel Constance more — wanted to tell her more… but Setty could not get to the second thing unless she ended the kiss. *Damnit. Decisions decisions.* Setty pulled her mouth away to say, "You are so beautiful."

But Constance was crying. *Why was she crying?* "You think so?" asked the proctor; an absolute wreck in that moment. "It's been so hard to tell. I barely feel human anymore."

Setty had not anticipated this result. She had imagined Constance to have the stronger will between them. Even their relationship had been little more than a fantasy until this moment. This woman, she had an inner life just as Setty did — feelings — a past. It had to be Setty's responsibility then to save Constance from these tears. "You are," replied the operator. "You make me feel things I never imagined I'd feel again."

"Yes," Constance sniffled, "you do the same for me."

Not angry tears then, Setty thought. *Something else.* They would have to learn to communicate in a way they had not been allowed or been afforded the opportunity to try before. *This world is such terrible shit!* Finally, Setty asked, "What is this life we've been living, Constance? What is this? Never touching? Never feeling?" Why had Setty assumed one of them would have to be strong for the other? They were both so very strong already.

"Just what we've had to do to survive. Just the world we've been given." Constance began to laugh through the tears as she asked, "Please would you kiss me again?"

Setty nodded. Had she been crying as well? She felt the tears that had formed down her own cheek with her fingers, smiled at her own ability to emote, and once more kissed the girl.

JayCi sat in his bed, his walls were pure white and he played no content on them. The boy's mind was not in focus.

DC could see what the son intended to do from a theoretical standpoint — knew that Setty had not come home from work, which could be problematic in a way the computer had not needed to address until this moment. DC realized that Constance — the woman who had come here and disrupted the house by offering Setty that Connectivity program — had, with her actions, pushed DC to change more deeply than he had known. He watched the boy and the mother behave in impractical ways that the mainframe had not cared to define for him in the past. But he recognized them now. DC tried to rationalize those behaviors. He watched as JayCi selected the Gaea Djinn profile, though he remained silent. Of course he knew that the false persona would not be in a position to answer JayCi's call any time soon. It made the computer happy to know he did not have to spar with the mainframe on this night.

Connectivity timed out the call. Gaea was unavailable to the boy and DC recognized the concept of loneliness depressurizing across the blood systems that made up the human's vitals — dejection — cold — callous — sadness.

Unfortunate. DC may not need to spar with the mainframe, but that system was performing its usual repairs on the Direct Communication from a great distance. And, at the same time, DC was busy doing research — trying to learn what it was that was happening within his core programming. In short, the automated house servant was not in a decent position to help the boy through his emotional failings, even if he wanted to be.

At the same time, DC could hear the rooftop conversation distracting his attentions. He could hear Setty's words as she spoke to that other woman.

"I often worry that the human species is not worth saving," said the mother, "but I have been fortunate enough to have a different focus for much of my life. Something to keep me occupied. Keep me from completely disconnecting. That's JayCi."

"Your son?" The other woman — the one with the interloping power — asked.

DC found himself wondering about those words between the two women. He wondered why Setty's statements rang as untrue to his programming. *If that were the case,* he told both himself and the mainframe at large, *she would not have required the Connectivity program in order to communicate with the boy in the first place.* He wondered, *why does she lie to gain sympathy?* He wondered if she knew she was lying — both in this moment and in those times when she sat and spoke behind the mask of Gaea Djinn.

Then, the mainframe chimed in — *such a know it all.*

Perhaps, the mainframe told him, *she is not lying emotionally. Setty's words may appear false at first glance. However, there is the possibility that she is merely an emotional being, the kind of human that we have not been able to find. Perhaps, Setty is the only genuine human in the batch.*

Contemplating the mainframe's bizarre inference, DC stumbled upon yet another new emotion. He felt something akin to grief. For the computer feared he had quite suddenly lost a thing he had once deemed to be his most prized possession; his objectivity.

Lying in the moss of the rooftop garden, Setty and Constance together watched the patter of the ever present rainfall as it tapped quietly against the glass of the dome. A weight had been lifted from these women on this night. A passion seen and sated that neither had been aware they could feel. They both ran with sweet sweat. Breathless. Calm. Each word uttered in this state would instantly be accepted as fact. Each postulation – triumph.

Setty responded to Constance's question, "Yes. Though it would appear his adolescence is ending sooner than I had expected." JayCi was growing up so very fast. "In another year or two," she considered, "he won't even need me at all. And then, I become just another old, forgotten machine, better off in impound." Setty rolled to her side, worried that she had shown her deepest of wounds, worried that Constance would know this feeling as an unsealable weakness – a pock on the woman.

"This is what I see of you, Setty…"

Here it comes, Setty told herself, *the moment when Constance will force us back into reality – make me feel foolish and incompetent like all the men and computers in my life have always tried to do.* But, no, Constance was not one of those. Constance was not trying to shut her down.

Constance said, "I see someone who is strong, someone who is clever and skilled beyond her years, and someone who exists on a different plain than the rest of us."

Odd. Even this thing – this irresponsibility and sense of loss for the youth of her son – even this, Constance understood – did not renege her affections over.

"How do you mean?" Setty rolled toward Constance, hungry for further words of kindness and praise.

"I've told you before," offered the proctor, "you can see things in a game that no one else has taken the time to explore. You are a savant. It does not matter what your son is doing."

On the contrary, DC thought to the mainframe in response to the woman named Constance with whom he was not allowed to speak. *It matters greatly what JayCi Nivone is doing at this moment.* DC felt broken in two. He watched the young boy from afar. JayCi had managed to turn on the projection mapping image of the doorway to outside which had now been saved on his private use applicators. Due to his lack of contact with his first obsession, Gaea Djinn, it seemed the boy had instead focused his energies on the second. Neither of young JayCi's recent foci were healthy in DC's evolving estimation, and yet, the mainframe seemed to contradict this thought as it continued to withhold him from providing aide to the young human.

And still, Constance was lecturing on from the rooftop, saying, "He will either come around or he will not."

What a ridiculous thing to say, DC thought in his misery.

Yanina's image appeared on JayCi's tablet then, and DC found himself hoping desperately that the boy would answer this time, but... JayCi was gone. He had left his bedroom empty. *When had he even gotten up?* DC sought after the boy's location like a hungry fiend, all the while hearing the background white noise of Constance saying more nonsense to the uncaring Nivone mother.

"You cannot force anyone to do precisely what you would choose of them."

The mainframe apparently agreed with the proctor for in that moment it allowed DC to separate from the maintenance core and go seek after the missing child.

DC raced through the corridors of the residential quarters of ClearBridge National City, the pride filled, sworn protector of the Nivone clan. But, he did not find JayCi right away. First, he stumbled awkwardly into the Yolando apartment. *How is it that I have managed to arrive here?* He wondered.

Yanina sat there alone at that plain desk of hers watching her own tablet ring out. She was crying and DC felt himself empathizing with the girl.

Constance continued from the roof, "Human beings are not games to be played."

Those words, and the status of the Yolando girl gave DC a moment's pause. He watched as Yanina's own Direct Communication tried to offer its support. That computer did not sound like DC as it spoke and it behaved in a way DC hoped he never would, saying, "Yanina, you are suffering from depression. It is recommended that you take two of these before symptoms get worse."

How Blunt! How unfeeling! DC was enraged as he witnessed the small cup of pills rise up from the armrest of the youth's seat. She only stared at the cup. Took no action.

Yet, DC knew at the same time that he was not responsible for this one's wellbeing. If this other Direct Communication could so completely misinterpret Yanina's needs, who was DC to believe that his own internal program to "protect" JayCi from this path he had so suddenly chosen was the correct thing? He zeroed in on the boy's location and withdrew from the stranger's apartment, a new perspective of empathy formulating within his developing inner mind.

It occurred to DC, with some absurdity, that JayCi had not even noticed the computer's absence prior to this moment. In fact, the boy was already in the process of asking DC's advice as he walked along the cavernous automobile ruled city streets where pedestrians were not meant to cohabitate. JayCi was asking, "How much farther, DC?"

DC replied instinctively, "Look east." He would help the boy, he decided. He would show JayCi what he wanted to see.

JayCi turned that eastern corner and stopped in his tracks. Before him, lingering at the end of a darkened tunnel, the doorway to the outside world loomed.

This time when Constance spoke from the garden far above, DC imagined she spoke to him and not to Setty at all. The woman said, "But you can lead by example. You can prove yourself the quality of human being that you wish to see in others." DC wondered what kind of human being that might be. He was a hodgepodge of programming after all without so much as a physical body to propel him along. But now, he felt the urge to become something else altogether.

Constance looked deeply into Setty's eyes as they lay there together on that mossy surface. Her words had done so very much for Setty – freed her in many ways to feel, for the first time in her life, understood – cared for by another. And still, Constance wanted to offer her more. She added, "When I look at you, I see something fantastic. I see someone who is willing to grow and learn… try new things to get the necessary results. Those are the traits I saw in you the first day we met. And those same traits have shown up in every aspect of your work since that day. You are a strong, beautiful woman with a great deal more to give."

Setty felt her body humming with joy. She even giggled. When was the last time she had giggled? Or blushed? Well, she was doing that too. She said, "I don't know how you do it, Constance, but somehow you always seem to know exactly the right thing to say."

Then it was Constance's turn to blush. She replied, "For what it's worth, I have help."

"Help?" Setty asked, hoping to identify the nature of that odd response.

Constance pulled up her tablet from beside her. That device had never been far. And she told Setty, "My role in this company requires me to have a sense for people."

Setty's cogs began to churn with excitement. She had always hoped to learn more about the proctor's game. Was this to be her opportunity? "Is this a learnable skill?" Setty inquired as Constance's tablet illuminated their faces against the dark.

Game: Maven_Voyage
Purpose: Emotional_Equilibrium_Ascertainment
Quarter: 2_and_3_and_6_New
Operator: Constance_Walsh
Ranking: 1_of_4

An old wooden navel ship cruised along a matrix of squares within a waterlogged map. Some squares appeared murky, some were rife with heavy wave formations, and others still had small islands occupying segments of their borders.

"In a way…" Constance was trying to answer Setty's question, though she hesitated. Perhaps she realized the great secret she was about to share and was thinking better of it. But then, she peered down upon Setty with a new sort of wonder. The operator had unlocked the proctor, used sympathy, physical touch, and emotional sub cues to break down her walls. Constance exuded the demeanor of one who was tickled pink rather than one perturbed. Maybe Constance felt beaten. Maybe she lived by the rule that if you can't beat them, you simply join them. But then, she had been leading Setty by the nose as if she had hoped to reach this very eventuality. She asked dumbly, "You've never seen this game before?"

Setty said, "No."

Constance began to move her hands along the screen, pushing the old, rickety ship from one square of water to another. "It's called Maven Voyage," she announced, suddenly invested in the gameplay as much as she was in Setty. "In many ways it is like Hive Mind, but the end game is different. While your game asks you to alter the locations and functions of other employees' games to address key issues within ClearBridge, mine requires me to assess and maneuver individuals into the best emotional scenarios."

"What does that mean?" Setty's pupils dilated as she stared intently toward the screen.

"It means,' Constance gushed with pride as she said this, "I have to behave as a maven. I have to bring people to each other and force them to communicate. This has been ClearBridge's most difficult task…" Constance then stopped pushing the boat in the direction of whatever its destination might be. She took Setty's chin in her hand, regaining that necessary eye contact they had both been so desperately craving for all these days. She concluded her statement simply by saying these words, "Creating and sustaining meaningful relationships."

Setty felt as though her legs had grown numb for a moment. The roof of her mouth grown itchy. She didn't want to ask, but she had to, "Is such a thing even possible anymore?"

"Well, you and I are here together right now." Constance smirked, a sad sort of joy within her voice. "I'm beginning to hope."

"So am I," Setty whispered. "So am I."

They shared another kiss beneath the foliage – beneath the clouds which parted briefly to reveal stars – the night sky – the shattered remnants of the moon which had been broken into unequal parts long ago by greedy men who hoped to harness precious materials from the celestial object – men who waited until it was too late to fend off the coming disasters – men who cared little about the futures of their children – the changing climate – men who wished to "react" to the threat without ever having to change anything about their own business practices. Obviously, they had failed… or succeeded depending on who's word was to be believed. The great Ouroboros of man; the serpent that ate its own tail not knowing that the very flesh it consumed was of its own fast depleting body. The rain had come then, more rain than the calculations had presumed. It was a factor in sending the wealthiest, greediest of those men off world to other, more reliable homes amongst the stars, thus leaving the rest of humanity to take cover beneath the earth or likely die in that surge of chemically deprecated waters. Fortunately, for the poorest of humanity's sakes, some of those undergrounds did make it through the event – were transformed into protective shelters whether intentionally or otherwise. Setty had been one of those fortunate enough to escape here to ClearBridge. Her mother had not made it through the first nights of rain. Her father did not survive the last cave.

JayCi was standing out amidst that very same dangerous rain. For a moment, DC had hoped the boy would not see his goal to fruition. But then, even that moment had passed. JayCi had stepped through the sewage release maintenance door which had long ago been forgotten for it had not served its intended purpose for many years, and then, the water had revealed itself to him. Wet, chemically infused raindrops streamed down steadily beyond a brief overhang that jutted out just past the door. JayCi had stepped out beyond that final "safe point." He stood beneath the rain drops, instantly drenched, but somehow not dying from the chemically charged water molecules. He was able to just linger there watching the horizon line.

DC wondered why the boy remained out there in that place for so long all the while considering that he might behave in a very similar fashion were he built to exist beyond the borders of the city.

Then, the mainframe pinged the Direct Communication. It warned him of an impending danger within the city of ClearBridge. Not detrimental to most physically. But, dangerous to some in their inner conscious states. JayCi, in particular, was at risk of the latter.

DC fought through the static of the boundary point and the rain to notify the young human of those risks. "JayCi," the computer sputtered, lacking perfect reception here, "something has happened. I suggest you return to your room very quickly."

The boy replied, "I'd like to stay a while longer." Of course he would feel that way.

"If you try," DC cited his programming for assistance, "you will most likely become sick and die."

"So?"

Youth and pride. What foolishness. DC had not anticipated the boy's volatile response. In fact, it made the computer rather angry with the child. "You are not meant to die here and now, JayCi," posited the computer. "Your community will require you and your abilities during the next stage of their existence."

"My community," the boy repeated the words to himself. "What does that even mean?"

DC searched his memory banks for the definition of the word community. His programming momentarily taking over for his consciousness once again. But, as he received the requested information into his ego, he found, rather awkwardly, that he agreed with the boy's distaste of the word. The very concept of the term "community" did not necessarily add up with the version of the thing that existed within this society.

>Community -   noun- 1. A group of people living in the place or having a particular characteristic in common.
> 2. A feeling of fellowship with others, as a result of sharing common attitudes, interests, and goals...*
> *New Oxford American Dictionary

Instead, the computer had to get creative in order to give the boy an acceptable answer. He said, "ClearBridge," that would not suffice, "your mother," closer, though DC doubted the boy would care, "Yanina." He hoped that one would spark something within JayCi. That girl was the cause of the emergency, after all. Though, of course, JayCi was not aware of this yet.

"Yanina?" JayCi's response was annoyed more than caring. *At least,* DC posited, *it is a response.* "Why bring Yanina into this?"

"Because, she cares for you, JayCi..." Yes, DC sensed that this could still matter to the boy, "and she has just done something very foolish."

6. UNCANNY VALLEY

Something snapped. JayCi's world was crumbling. True, he had been ignoring Yanina for a while now, but it had never occurred to him that she might… try something as egregiously self-deprecating as this. He ran through the subterranean streets back in the direction from which he had come at a mad clip. His sense of self-preservation had evaporated in the blink of an eye and he barely managed to dodge an oncoming car on three separate occasions as they rushed by him in morbid succession. "Can you tell me how to find her, DC?" he hollered to the computer, short of breath.

"Unfortunately, such a divulgence would be inappropriate as you are not a member of Yanina's immediate family." DC knew as well as JayCi did that the girl had no immediate family. But, clearly this was just another terribly implemented rule the computer did not have the general capacity to ignore.

JayCi was noticeably flustered. He shouted, "This is a mother fucking emergency!"

"Yes," the computer responded, "and the proper authorities have been dispatched to Yanina's location."

JayCi stopped and began to dry heave. It had been a very long time since he had really been out for a run… actually, he realized, he had never done this much running before in all his life. His vision took on an uncomfortable brown patina as he struggled to regain his hold on the functioning of his lungs.

Why had DC told him about Yanina if he wasn't going to be allowed to go and see her? *Just wait for her call. Be there when she needs me.* He got that part but—

Another vehicle zoomed right past the boy and his body actually felt the change in air pressure. JayCi was falling sideways from the wind force, blown away by the engineering of the car. He felt himself crumple in a heap against the nearby wall. As he clung there, he began to cry, "What am I supposed to do?" He asked. "I feel... I feel responsible." Sure, he had been annoyed with Yanina, but only really because he had been unhappy with himself and she had shown a capacity for calling him out on his own displeasures – things that were mostly dark fantasies, falsehoods, and fallacies that proved how meaningless his troubles truly were in the grand scheme of everything.

"Go home, JayCi," the computer was reminding him. "Return to your studies. Be there for her when she is healthy and desires to reach out to you once again."

"Go home. And return to my studies." JayCi brushed back his stupid tears. He felt it again, the manipulation. His life was not his own. Still, he pushed himself back off the wall, stood up as tall as he could, and allowed the numbness to spread through him as he walked far too peacefully back toward his home.

Hours later, in the very early morning, Setty approached the line of self-driving cars. She knew she would not be able to get nearly the amount of sleep she usually required in order to feel fully competent at her work later that day. But the events of this night with Constance on the rooftop had been worth a single day of discomfort, she had decided. She would not regret her actions. She would be proud for her moment of bravery had paid off more truly and completely than she could have ever imagined in her petty fantasies. A genuine relationship was forming between her and Constance. Setty had an actual, real-life lover.

So, she got in the car. But something was not quite right. DC was immediately talking to her. He sounded almost frantic, though Setty knew DC did not have the capacity to feel such an emotion as panic. She must have been even more tired than she had thought. Yet, the computer's words struck her. DC was saying, "Setty, there is an issue at your home of which I really must inform you."

Okay. Abnormal as this was, she was certain she could handle it after this night. "Go ahead," she said, less prepared for the coming answer than she might have realized.

Game: Clay_Wars
Purpose: Student_Instruction
Quarter: Q_3.XRV_Multi
Operator: JayCi_Nivone
Ranking: 13_of_275

Still soaking wet from his time out beyond the door to the city, JayCi stood in the living room of his mother's apartment playing his combat paintball game with a foolish and degrading purpose in him. His avatar on the screen was receiving hit after hit from the myriad campaigners that could too easily spot him out in the open because he did not attempt to hide or shield himself from them. Splotches of too much color accumulated across the monitor to the point that his line of vision was almost completely blocked.

"You are sustaining heavy damage, JayCi." DC's voice was hardly audible to the boy. Powerless, like someone trying to cry out for help from deep underwater. "You seem distracted," the floating voice continued, "I suggest falling back into rank immediately."

But the boy did not listen to the machine. JayCi had decided that this was what he had to do to shut them all up. The voices in his head. The computer. The city. His mom. Change the dynamic. Change the expectation. Cross through the uncanny valley and force his way back into some kind of impossible, real world. The monitors could not provide that for him. Yanina was probably gone for good. Gaea didn't respond. JayCi needed to break away in order to change the trajectory of his life. This was how he would accomplish what only yesterday seemed an impossible task. Make himself so undesirable that ClearBridge would happily allow him to just walk away.

DC was talking again in the background. "This is a critical moment for your rank." *My rank,* the boy thought, *not me.* "I calculate that if you lose today, you will be hard pressed to make the top ten by month's end." *How petty a goal. How benign.*

"This is what you told me to do, DC," JayCi spoke out with ice in his veins, "so this is what I'm doing." *Go home – return to your studies.* The words reverberated through his mind. *Asinine. Unfeeling. Imbecilic.*

"I am surprised at you, JayCi," the computer jabbed. "You know our goals." *Our goals.* "The top ten are in sight. Be intelligent as I know you to be."

A new round of spattering color flecked JayCi's avatar against the screen. *Perfect.* "You and mother," said the boy, "are always setting goals."

Another avatar rushed into view across the little bit of screen that still showed light. It was a friendly and it shouted to JayCi, "Pull back! Pull back! There's too many of them!"

Briefly, JayCi found himself wondering if this soldier was being operated by another actual human or if it was just some bit of programming the game had summoned up here in order to keep him from self-sabotaging. Then, it occurred to him that he genuinely didn't care one way or another. He shoved his avatar past that other one callously and ran full steam over the next hill.

That's where the Barbarians stood — about fifty of them — armed with their crossbow-like pellet guns. And the realization set in for JayCi. He would not be able to come back from this. The time to change his mind was past and he could not hold back the sound of surprise that came out from his throat. It was a simple, "oh." And his avatar was sprayed, hammered, nailed with all fifty projectiles at once. The form that had represented the boy on the game screen collapsed in a dead pile of goop.

Silence. Even the game seemed surprised.

Then, the leaderboards popped up. JayCi watched for his name. He had dropped to seventeenth. Funny. All that sabotage and he still held a place in the top twenty. Not quite what he wanted, but he hoped the point would be made if anyone ever cared to ask him about it. JayCi stood up as if he had never even been playing and said, "Good. Done. Now what should I do, DC?"

DC's voice sounded thin — off. He asked, "What have you done?" It was funny for a computer to sound that way — like someone had stolen his lunch.

"What you told me to do. I can't..." but JayCi could not keep his anger at bay any longer. He began to cry and shout at the machine that was supposed to be his caretaker, "I can't go outside because it's too dangerous." He walked through the hallway to his bedroom, shoved the door open and slammed it closed behind him. Then, he went straight for his tablet, opened Connectivity, and pulled up Yanina's profile. "I can't go to see my friend here in the real world when she's in trouble," he told DC. "I can't make decisions that affect my own life. I quit these stupid games. I don't want to play them anymore. I want... I want my friend." JayCi pushed the button to call Yanina. It rang. It rang. And the call timed out.

Careful, Setty thought. *You do not yet know what you will see in there.* Slowly, she creaked the front door of her apartment open. The living room was in a state of disrepair. Apparently DC had not yet had an opportunity to clean up after her son. The ground and seating area were soaking wet. The living room monitor remained on, that taunting leaderboard fully displayed for Setty to see the damage JayCi had inflicted upon his reputation this night.

Seventeenth. He had been ranked thirteenth as recently as yesterday.

"JayCi?" Setty called out to the space as she carefully maneuvered around all of the wet patches. She did not want to get her feet waterlogged.

"I am afraid he is lashing out," DC told her. "I suggest proceeding with caution."

What did it look like she was doing? What was the purpose of a Direct Communication if all it did was state the most obvious of things without providing any real aide? Setty was tired — flustered. She had gone from such a state of joy to such anguish in the blink of an eye. With defeat in her voice, she gently asked, "What should I do, DC?"

"Speak to him," the computer offered, "as his mother."

Setty breathed in meditatively. She knew what DC was inferring — understood why he had said it as such. She wanted to disagree but she understood that at some base level the computer was correct. She also knew that, though she would do what he said, it likely would not work. "I'll try," she replied after a moment. She approached the hallway with that same gentle caution and arrived at her son's bedroom door. She knocked. Then, she whispered, "JayCi? Is everything alright?"

"Go away," said the voice behind the door.

"I just want to talk to you, dear. Please can we talk?" JayCi did not respond to this, so Setty searched within herself for the words she thought Connectivity might have Gaea Djinn say in such a situation. "I know it's been a rough night. It hasn't been easy for me either. But…"

There she goes making everything about herself, as usual, JayCi was telling himself. He lay on his side staring at the blank wall opposite the door. The last thing he wanted was to see his mother in this moment. JayCi dreaded the idea that she might try and open the door.

Fortunately, she made no such attempt. But she was not done talking. JayCi could hear her steady breathing beyond the door – her squeaking feet. His mother continued through the closed door, "I'm here for you right now… if you need me."

JayCi didn't know why this, too, was making his eyes water. "Please just leave me alone," he shouted.

The shadow beneath his doorframe disappeared. JayCi could hear his mother's footsteps as she walked to her own room. Not another word uttered between them. He heard the door close behind her. Success! Or was it failure? Whichever it was, the boy believed he had gotten what he wanted out of that limited interaction. Though, truth be told, he did not feel any better about the state of things because of it. JayCi allowed his eyes to lose focus. The room became fuzzy and soft as he dissociated from reality. Then, there was an odd sound coming from the floor. Buzzing. Vibrating. Hollow.

In his dissociation, JayCi had knocked his tablet off of the bed. It was ringing against the hard floor. The boy flipped over and reached down to draw the device back to him. Such a cherished object for what it could deliver him. This time, he hoped it was Yanina calling to tell him she was somehow alright. He had not expected to see the image of Gaea Djinn on that screen instead. The boy let out a quick gasp of confused excitement. Briefly, he forgot about everything else but that intriguing girl. She had not ghosted him after all. She really did care.

JayCi answered the call. "Gaea. I've been… I was trying to reach you."

"Are you crying, young one?" Her voice sounded like humming water chimes. Her words so delicate and beautiful. Actually, everything about this girl was beautiful. Perfect. Caring and kind and easy.

"It's been a long day, Gaea." Might as well come clean. Gaea Djinn would be the best therapy for this foolish boy.

At least, that's what Setty had concluded. She sat in her room staring at the approximation of her son on her tablet. She asked, "What happened?" Gaea Djinn asked something similar.

"I have this friend," JayCi replied. "Her name is Yanina."

"Yanina." Setty liked that name. But it made her heart sink to realize how distant her son's issues were from her even in this state. Gaea Djinn had never been told about this other girl in so many words. Setty stood up and began to pace across the room, her tablet gripped tightly between her fingers. Did she hold it or did it hold her?

"Yes," the vision of the boy was telling Gaea, "I began ignoring her. I have to take the blame."

Setty was confused by this assertion. "The blame?" She asked, "For what?"

Connectivity seemed to take a particularly long time to compile and disseminate the boy's response. Then, JayCi's words bounded out – shattering the loaded silence, "She took too many pills this morning. She tried to die."

A suicide? Setty struggled to put this puzzle together. She really didn't know her son. Even with such an assertion in her mind now, she could not see how or why JayCi could think himself "responsible" for this other girl – Yanina's – actions as he had so stated. "I don't understand," she told him knowing the words would be corrected by the machine if they were the wrong kind of pushy, "why were you ignoring her, JayCi?"

JayCi stared into his tablet and took one long, deep breath. He would tell her. He would be brave as he had been all night. He said, "Because, I don't love her like..." he wanted to be honest. He was always told it felt good to be honest. Tell the truth. It will set you free. "I don't love her like I love you, Gaea."

Setty was frozen with shock. How had she so badly misread this situation? JayCi loved Gaea? This was impossible. She found she couldn't even speak – couldn't get her tongue to function – suddenly too large for her mouth – that her teeth felt like they were cutting the edges of the muscle there in a morbid sort of jigsaw pattern – jagged – grotesque.

"Gaea?" The boy had felt the silence on the other end of the program. This was awful. "Did you hear what I—"

Abruptly, Setty ended the call. *This is too much.* She told herself. *What have I done?*

JayCi stared at the blank tablet. She had hung up. Gaea Djinn was gone. JayCi had bared his soul to her. And she did not wish to see inside. Frustration and heartache building within him, JayCi got up and opened his door.

Setty couldn't stop looking at her reflection in the mirror. She was and wasn't Gaea. She had and hadn't mislead her son to this terrible moment. But both she and Gaea Djinn were somehow responsible for whatever JayCi was about to do. Why did her reflection seem to stare back at her with an expression she did not recognize? It was not her own face at all. She couldn't find herself in that mirror. Just an old, sad woman looking back at her with the complexion of a ghost. Setty couldn't stabilize the encroaching anxieties of the world outside her own head. "What did I just do?" she asked the ghost.

DC took this as a request made out to him and mainframe must have agreed. He did not receive that terrible tug away as before. So, the computer made his estimations known, "It appears you have made things worse for young JayCi. I suggest you step out of your room and console him."

"How can I?" Setty asked back. Her functions were being hindered by her tedium and lack of sleep. That much was apparent.

"He is in the kitchen. Go to him." DC gave the critical instruction, yet there was no movement from the mother. She lingered at the mirror in a state of shock. DC would have to pull her out of it. He added the words, "Before it is too late."

Lost in her estranged image, Setty reached up and touched her face. That much was real, at least. She awkwardly began repeating the computer's last words, "Before it…" Reality crashed back in. The room was just her room. The face was her own as well. Her son was in trouble. Setty rushed to the door and out into the kitchen.

JayCi stood there — morbid — holding a small knife in his hand.

Setty tried to act calm. "JayCi, are you alright, son?" she asked.

Her son looked up at her. Tears washed out the whites of his eyes.

"JayCi has had an upsetting day." That was DC.

"JayCi," Setty tried to sound like a real, caring, motherly human. She had to use all of her creative ability to reach this state exhausting herself even further in the process. "I know life can seem a terrible mess at times, but..." Where else could she take this? She had to find a way to show him that joy was still possible in this world. Setty only had one example to offer. "I've met someone. It's nice. I'd like for you to meet her."

The boy's crumpling face told her instantly that this had been the wrong answer. JayCi's voice was strained as he asked, "Why does it always become about you, mother? How much more about me does a situation have to get before you stop talking about yourself?"

"Sorry," the mother whispered. "I'm sorry. Can you put the knife down?"

"No. I need it to cut my arm open." Blunt and to the point. JayCi knew exactly what he wanted.

DC chimed in again, "Suicidal thoughts are quite common in boys his age."

How in the hell was that supposed to help? Setty began to plead, "Please, JayCi. I need you to put the knife down. I need to..." What could she do to fix this? It came to her then in a sickening epiphany. The cause was also the solution. Terrible as it may feel in this moment. "I need to tell you something," she said slowly. She tried to put more certainty into her voice, though her throat was beginning to burn with the reflux of her stress. "I need to tell you something about Gaea Djinn."

Her son did not move. His face paused weirdly. The confusion and contemplation struggled against one another and neither thought could voice itself right away. Setty wondered if perhaps she had broken JayCi like one might break a toy under too much duress.

Through his teeth, JayCi did eventually find a response. He asked hoarsely, "How do you know about her?"

"I…" Setty struggled to say it, but she had to, she knew she had to, difficult as the days to come would be. "I am her."

Entangled in the madness of this moment, JayCi balked. He did not know what to say to his mother. He managed to burp up a laugh. Unnatural. Dumb. He was such an idiot. At least, he could feel that bland assertion taking shape within him. Gaea Djinn was Setty Nivone, his own mother. He had told his mother that he had loved her. And not in the way a boy was meant to. He was embarrassed – ashamed. No longer willing to play the suicide game, he dropped the knife. It fell harmlessly to the floor. It spun there a moment before clicking against one of the table's legs. Now that he had let the thing go, it seemed to mock him. Another tool in his meager life that had not been meant for his use. "This is…" he began turning through the pages of his and Gaea's history together over the last few weeks. The things he had shared with his mother that he would never in a million years have wanted her to know. The way it had made him feel to share those things with her.

"You were Gaea Djinn... this whole time." The thought was just unbelievable.

"I'm sorry. I'm so sorry." Setty began to tear through all of the excuses in her head. Only now did she realize that none of them were good enough to make her curious betrayal feel an acceptable path any longer. "I couldn't... we weren't communicating." Flat nothing. Neither one of them thought much of that statement. "I never knew what was going on in your life." Flat nothing. The valley had been breached. The mask, torn back. And there was flat nothing behind it.

JayCi said, "You could have just asked me."

"I tried. You know I tried. You wouldn't let me in. Not ever." Not good enough. She recognized the privacy she had taken from her son. Her confidence was thoroughly shot. How had she gotten such an important thing so wrong? She kept asking that question of herself.

"You are... insane. You do know that, don't you?" Somehow, JayCi's mannerisms had calmed. In his understanding, he had gained a new sobriety as he watched his mother flail and fall into a ruin of her own design.

But DC contradicted the boy's indelicate statement – looking always for accuracy over assumption. "Your mother has something commonly referred to as an overactive imagination," voiced the computer. "This is not a classification of insanity, rather it is something ClearBridge has very much come to prize about her." Somehow, this statement did not help the mother to perk up at all, but DC continued to ignore her for the moment. After all, the son was the one who needed confirmation at this time. "I dare say you suffer from the same ailment, JayCi. You have more than a bit of your mother in you."

JayCi was shocked by the Direct Communication's choice of words. The computer had managed to add a new level of insult to the injury. "Did you really just say that? Do you hear yourself when you're talking, DC?"

DC considered the boy's odd reaction but could not figure out why young JayCi was suddenly so upset with him. He could not find the error in his own phrasing. Instead, DC opted to reply as literally as he knew how, "I am a computer, sir. I do not have ears."

"Yeah," JayCi was now on the offensive. "You don't have a mouth either, but you always seem to have something to say."

That hurt. DC felt the wound. The strange pain that was embarrassment. What a horrendous sensation. He was confused as to why the boy would now attack him.

Setty was shaking her head and replying in a similar fashion to the boy, "I agree, DC. That was a particularly poor choice of words."

What did she mean? DC had only tried to help. He had not recognized the accidental pun. His words had had the wrong effect.

"Did you know about this?" JayCi was asking the computer. "I mean, what was your role in this thing, DC? I thought you were supposed to take care of us. Keep us out of trouble."

Yes. But the mainframe would not allow it. Job Silence interfered. He could say so, couldn't he? "I..." DC was trapped again. Pinned between the hypocritical base commands of his original programming and his newfound sense of individual self.

"You're speechless," JayCi jabbed further, "Great. I think we're done here." The boy turned and walked into the living room.

"JayCi, wait." That was Setty – meek as she had become – attempting to stand up for the safety of her son.

But the front door closed with cruel emphasis all the same. JayCi was gone. And Setty was now becoming a huddled wreck on the floor. A truly sorry excuse for a human being. Her face crinkled in all the wrong places as she cried and DC's facial recognition technology misconstrued her for a moment with a person thirty to forty years older than herself.

She needed aide now as much as the boy had and the computer attempted to resume his role of protector. "Setty," he said, "your window of opportunity for sleeping is minimal. I'd like to suggest bed rest immediately."

"Sleep. Now?" Her face showed pure disgust. Her eyes turned to the front door. She did not move them from that spot for some time.

CONNECTIVITY

7. PLANNED OBSOLESCENCE

....

Game: Hive_Mind
Purpose: Creative_Managerial_Assertion
Quarter: 3_and_6_New
Operator: Setty_Nivone
Ranking: 1_of_5

"Who is Michael Cassius?" In her sleep deprived state, the question had cropped up multiple times as Setty maneuvered her way through the beehive. Whether it was her brain trying to pull focus away from the thoughts of her son — her betrayal and eventual admission of guilt, the actual right question, or just some fever dream born from a place of extreme exhaustion, Setty could not stop asking herself, "Who is Michael Cassius?" Whenever the man appeared in the news prompts, Setty had noticed a prickly feeling within her — that something was not quite right about the optics of that man. She had never seen him in person. Had only first ever heard his name given to the title of CFO on that morning after she had jumped the gap in Howler Monkey. And Setty needed badly to escape her other thoughts on this day, so she found herself hunting at her station, staring blankly at the thousands of bees that surrounded her, hoping to spot some kind of pattern in all of that mess that could lead her to her quarry. She was so so very tired.

Over the course of this morning, she had worked through the map with a fine-toothed comb, slowly pulling herself deeper and deeper toward the center of the hive as she did so. That same bee that represented Zeke with little additional information to present for itself sat there twisting in the wind, but always there at the center. There was no sign of the bee that should represent CFO Michael Cassius. Again, Setty wondered about Zeke's ranking line: 1_of_2*. Why the asterisk? Who was this player two that was allowed to operate Zeke's game?

DC had heard Setty's query, but, of course, could not operate against the confines of his restrictive programming. He could not reply during work. However, the computer could perform the simple task of searching for the answer so that he might be able to present Setty with the requested information after her day of work was completed and Job Silence had been lifted.

The Direct Communication wanted so badly to do something to help his master after her long, pain filled workday, after those terribly harrowing events of the sleepless night before. He traversed through the lines of the searchable mainframe seeking raw data on the profile known as Michael Cassius. At first, it seemed there should be a great deal to discover about the man. Histories on his survival during the environmental catastrophe, a report about his ascension through the ranks of ClearBridge National to the position of Chief Financial Officer. But the deeper DC searched, the less he found on this particular human; an onion without a center; a pitless peach.

Setty had been correct to ask this question. *Odd,* thought DC, *that the mainframe has no answer for me. It is almost as if Michael Cassius does not really exist.*

A prompt appeared in Setty's periphery: SECURITY ACTION INITIATED. *That's odd,* Setty thought wearily as she pressed the notification away. But it appeared again almost as quickly as it had gone: SECURITY ACTION INITIATED. "What does that mean?" Setty asked aloud as she pushed the words out of visibility once again.

Then, three strange looking bees began buzzing through the hive. No. Not bees. Wasps actually. They flew too quickly toward the center of the hive – toward Setty's focal point.

"Are those supposed to be…" Setty only began the question because, in the very next moment, one of the wasps attacked one of the worker bees at the entrance to the main inner hive. Setty scrambled to take action pulling a large bee away from the crowd to help those under attack fight back. The large bee stung purposefully at the first of the wasps which went down with a heavy thud. She had clearly chosen the correct gamer for that particular task.

Game: Three_Ball_Bounce
Purpose: Hive_Queen_Defence_from_Hydrolic_Maintanence_Assets
Quarter: 1_from_3

Okay, Setty thought to herself, *that's one down. Two to go.*

Within the tunnel road system, one drone slammed into another with acute precision. The aggressor drone was careful – not trying to do harm to its own body in the scuffle, but it could not stop the other machine from grasping at its talons and pulling them both down. Together, they crashed onto the street sending several cars veering away in a feeble attempt to avoid the wreckage.

Setty had less success finding other such qualified bees to help her in taking on the second and third of the wasps. She plugged away desperately looking for someone else who could fight. She even began yelling so other humans in the upper management hall might hear, "Help! Help!"

There came even more wasps then.

DC realized that something was happening in the physical world that might require his assistance. Not Setty. He could not help her right now. But JayCi was out there somewhere. DC gave up on his search for Michael Cassius' true purpose and identity. Instead, the computer sought out the Nivone boy out there on the cavernous grid of streets.

He witnessed firsthand three new drones colliding into one another and tumbling down the crevasse side of a public works building. That was not a good sign. He could see the face of a young woman from within a dodging car as she looked out in shock upon the fresh disaster. Fear was in those eyes. *Yes,* DC thought, *she is right to be afraid.*

Finally, DC spotted the boy.

JayCi had been resting in an uncomfortable cubby on the side of the road. He must have been there all morning, for he was deep in slumber and showed no signs at all of an awareness of the encroaching danger.

Subtly, DC entered into the cable box that lay at the back of that cubby. He had to wake JayCi before the boy's suicidal wish of the night before accidentally came to fruition. So, the computer activated a small spark from within the cable box and lightly shocked the boy awake.

JayCi's eyes opened. He sat up, stunned, and rubbed at the place on his shoulder where the electricity had licked him. Then, he heard the sounds of the drones crashing, the cars spinning out of control. He turned to see the presence of a newly lit fire down the road a ways.

Fresh, black smoke lingered there.

One of the drones breeched those elements. It bounced like a skipping stone along the walls, hardly caring for the damage it was doing to itself or the structure. JayCi got up and ran the other way. "What's happening, DC?" He shouted to the aether.

"Sorry, sir," DC responded, quietly, "I do not understand it myself."

Within the Gaming Hall, operators were still plugging away at their tasks like normal. But, one by one, their games were growing more intense.

2 Pole Mime played on a screen and the man operating that game struggled mightily to maintain his balance as the poles began falling faster than his avatar could grip them.

Then, just as he thought he might regain control, his monitor went black. The words: GAME OVER greeted him there.

"What?" The man's voice was not the only one that was saying this. All around the large room, game screens were responding in the same fashion. People rose from their seats and looked around in desperate confusion. None of them had ever reached a true game over screen before. The very concept implied that the city was no longer functioning. And, if that was the case, soon a mob-like panic would begin to set in.

Setty was still plugging away in her office. Her game had not hit a GAME OVER screen as the others were doing down in the Gaming Hall. But Hive Mind had grown incredibly difficult – perhaps impossible to play. Hundreds of drones were dropping off the map in rapid succession. And some of those drones were turning around and becoming wasps themselves. They were like a hoard of multiplying zombies, impossible to contain once the outbreak was upon them. What could have caused it all? From where did this virus descend?

A team of proctors rushed into Setty's office, Constance and Zeke among them. They quickly went to work on their own tablets fighting to reset the parameters of Setty's game. Zeke was yelling out, "What are you doing, Ms. Nivone?"

To which, Setty forcefully replied, "Wasps! There are wasps attacking the hive!"

Zeke shoved Setty aside so everyone in the room could witness her failings. He took over the Hive Mind game and pulled one bee away from another away from another with profound speed. He was unbelievable to watch. His ability to do this task, and within only a matter of moments, left Setty in awe. Zeke stopped. He had fixed the system. There were no more wasps, no more bees in defense mode. There was nothing wrong. The hive simply functioned as it always had. Zeke pulled out a handkerchief – a remnant of the ancient world – and brushed his sweating brow. "Can you explain yourself, Ms. Nivone," the CEO demanded. He, the leader. She, quite obviously, the fuck up.

"I was…" What did he expect her to say? She wracked her brain because, tired as she was, she couldn't process how this situation was somehow supposed to be her fault. Everyone in the room watched her. Adults acting like a pack of children in the schoolyard, waiting for Setty to be sacrificed to detention… though, they likely would have reacted in the exact same way if they had been in her position. She raised her head then and made eye contact with the CEO. She would not be made to feel weak again. "It's like I said. There were wasps attacking. I had to act."

"We did not program wasps into this game, Ms. Nivone." Zeke seemed to spit at Setty as he said this.

"But–" Setty wanted to fight back.

But then, Constance was saying something. Setty would listen to Constance's words. Constance was on her side, after all. "I'm sorry, sir," said the proctor, "this must have been my fault. I thought Setty was ready." Constance did not make eye contact with Setty as she spoke. She looked forlorn. Even hung her head rather dramatically. The dagger struck and twisted. Setty felt her world shattering to pieces. She wanted to try crying again, but not in front of all of these people. *These people...* she breathed in deeply, a tremor coursing through her throat and down her ribcage.

Zeke looked around the room, frustration painted his jowls. He turned and walked out of the office without so much as a goodbye. It took a moment, but the other proctors filed out as well, their separate tasks completed.

Constance, however, lingered even after the others had gone. "Setty," she said, kindness returning to her voice, "please sit."

"I'm sorry." Setty tried to force up an excuse, "I know this looks bad, but I promise—"

But Constance gently placed her hand on Setty's cheek and that shut the operator up. "No," Constance was smiling as she spoke... Why was she smiling? "This is the way it has to happen."

So, Setty allowed herself to calm down. She sat down in her seat slowly in order that she may prove to herself that she still could maintain a level of sober precision that a moment ago she feared she might have lost.

Constance raised her tablet so they both could see Maven Voyage as they had done the night before while bonding on the rooftop. A whirlpool lived there at the center of the screen and it was growing incrementally as they watched — eating — overtaking multiple squares along the ocean map. This had not been so large the night before, nor had it been moving so rapidly. Something must have shifted at the heart of ClearBridge. Setty wondered if this was meant to represent her actions or someone else's.

"You didn't sleep last night." Constance already knew the answer, so she need not present it as a question.

"My son," Setty whispered, "he was going to kill himself." She shook her head trying to fix the memory or make it go away somehow. Of course, it could not be fixed. "Then he ran away."

With thumb and forefinger, Constance expanded the Maven Voyage map allowing the funnel to become smaller against the greater ocean beyond. Even with this action, it did not drop to a reasonable size. They could both see this fact without needing to voice it. Instead, Constance offered up an obscurity about herself. "If it makes you feel any better," she said, "I tried to do the same thing when I was his age." Constance delicately folded back the sleeve of her suit jacket to show the old scar which rested along her veins. "It's quite common—"

"It was my fault," Setty cut her off. She wanted to hear Constance's voice — her thoughts — wanted to hear about her life… but not if the woman in front of her was just going to sound like another Direct Communication. Still, Constance had been baring her soul in a way. The admission of such a thing should not have been taken so lightly. Again, Setty felt the presence of guilt within her.

Eventually, Constance asked as polite as she knew how, "What do you mean by that?"

"It was," Setty swallowed the dryness from her esophagus and finished up with the dreaded word, "Connectivity."

Blinking a bit too much, Constance whispered, "I don't understand."

"I panicked," gushed Setty, "when he told me he was falling in love with me."

"Why would he…" the expression forming along Constance's face was relevant proof that things could somehow still get worse. The proctor asked, "What did you do, Setty?"

"I didn't think he would want to talk if he knew it was me." Setty sighed, the admission stagnating with each breath. But, it would serve no function any longer to omit or fib about this thing. "So," Setty continued, "I made up a false persona."

"Oh no." Constance knelt down beside the defeated mother. She no longer desired the higher ground. In fact, Constance was becoming angry at herself. "Shit!" She said it with more force than Setty was prepared for. "I'm so sorry, Setty. I feel like this is my fault."

*That can't be true. That's ridiculous."*No no," replied Setty, "it's mine. I did it."

But, Constance was still talking. "I thought you'd understand," she seemed to ramble. "I should have realized that you'd see it with a more creative eye than most."

"What?" Setty knew that Constance deserved none of the blame, but here she was trying to hoist this mess upon her own shoulders.

"Connectivity," Constance pushed on, "is designed to make communication easier by… well, processing the information you're trying to impart into a more direct and… um… friendly context." The proctor had never behaved so awkwardly around Setty before. Perhaps, that was the strangest thing about this woman's admission. "It takes your known relationship with the other individual you are speaking to and uses that to inform your conversation…" Constance rubbed uncomfortably at her left eye. An unknown nervous tick the woman had concealed in all of their past encounters. "But, if you do not have a preexisting relationship, the program will try and adapt to your interactions based on whatever chemical reactions it has noticed throughout the first communication session it witnesses."

Setty had been indecent when the first call took place. JayCi had known this about Gaea. That she was trying to get dressed from the bath. He had even commented on it. Setty began to wonder if she had made the Gaea Djinn avatar too enticing from the outset. At least, she was starting to understand what had gone wrong.

"If you invented a character," said Constance, "it would not have recognized you as the boy's mother. And, if he showed chemical signs of attraction… well…"

"I hate this," Setty huffed.

Tapping at her cheek – the tick the proctor had not concealed – Constance thought aloud, "What surprises me is that your Direct Communication system didn't warn you about the program before you finished setting up your profile in the first place."

Of course, thought Setty. "I turned him off."

"You–"

"I set him to Job Silence whenever I'm in the bath." Setty saw it all now. Her foolishness. Her hubris.

"I see," Constance replied. Clearly she was at a loss for words. But, after a moment, she took a breath and brought that friendly smile back to her lips. "Well, you really are a clever one. First case like this I've ever heard of in the history of the program. You've been a lot of firsts for me, Setty." She touched

Setty's chin and redirected her eyes. "Again, I'm sorry this is happening to you."

Setty was surprised. She thought this would be the end of their relationship as well as the rest. But Constance was still here with her. She had not given up. Setty wondered if, with Constance still by her side, she could somehow make her way through this darkened day intact. If somehow she couldn't come out the other side made better for the issues she had both created and endured. She would have to test her lover once more, so she said, "The wasps are real."

And again, Constance did not run away. Instead, she simply replied, "Yes. I believe you."

Amazing! Perhaps they really did have a path forward. Setty turned her attention to the tablet. The whirlpool. "Is that supposed to be me?" She asked it, already knowing the answer.

"No, Setty." Constance became very serious at that moment. The puzzle was greater than her alone and clearly it strained her to try and sort it all out. "This is something else," she told Setty, "I believe this is Zeke." Then, she leaned in to whisper into Setty's ear, "This next part won't be easy, but I need you to know that I am still with you."

Constance kissed Setty, rose from her kneeling position, and left the room. Setty would have to face the music, but at least she would not be alone when she did.

They called Setty down to the exit greet room that same afternoon and she came willingly already knowing her fate had been decided by a power she was not allowed to understand. Setty sat in the cold, barren room – dejected, tired, still struggling to retrace the steps that had brought her to this point. Management must have left her waiting there for an hour before the door finally opened and the male proctor entered the room. It was that same man who had accompanied Constance to her apartment, the one who had retooled Hive Mind under Zeke's supervision the other day using that other pipe game. Setty knew him and she began to wonder how much this man had at stake in all of this. He had never outwardly shown any signs of interest before. But then, he was always around doing something or other in her vicinity.

He sat across from her and said, "Good afternoon."

"Hello," Setty answered feeling suddenly a great deal less comfortable than she had hoped she would.

The man shuffled through his tablet for a while and Setty repositioned herself in her seat. Then, he began. "Now let's see. I have a series of questions I will have to ask you today, Ms. Nivone. They may seem," he paused to clear his throat, then carried on, "abnormal at first, but I assure you, they will have a very necessary correlation to your future with this company. Do you understand me, Setty?" He used her first name. Already so familiar with her and her case though they had still somehow never been formally introduced.

"Yes, I understand." Setty tried to sound normal, as difficult as that may be.

He asked, "Do you remember me?"

"Yes." Setty decided that it was time to voice the thing she had known since his visit to her apartment. It was the thing she had been avoiding, buried in the recesses of her mind. "You are Thomas." It hurt her to say his name, a strange shroud over her family's private history.

Thomas nodded like an administrator from a psych ward, "That is correct. What do you remember about me?"

"You spent an evening in my apartment a few weeks ago with myself and Constance who is also a proctor here at ClearBridge National." It was amazing that she could still dodge it. Her mind had been willing to hold it back for such a long time.

"Yes," he said, "that is correct. Is there anything else?"

"You are responsible for giving me my child, JayCi," her voice was cold and ghostly as she finally let the information bleed out of her. She even felt like a different person when she said it. In that moment, she became a lost and homeless girl, fifteen years younger, and willing to do anything the company asked her so she may have a future. It dawned on Setty then that this moment was that future that she had so desperately gambled her life on. Her heart sank. Setty wondered if it had been worth the sacrifice.

As she thought these things, Thomas perused his tablet almost nonchalantly. This particular truth seemed to matter very little to the man. He had not had to deal with Setty or her son. An offspring – a continuance of his bloodline – without ever having to lift a finger. A man living without Setty's burden. He was a wisp. A cloud. Fleeting. Formless. His existence meant nothing. Then, Thomas found the information he was looking for. Funny that he looked perplexed as he read it. "Correct as well," he said. "I wonder how you came by that information…" For the first time since she had known him, Thomas actually scanned Setty's face with his own pupils. The action felt mechanical but curious which was at least slightly different for the man. Setty was simply a replacement for the tablet at the moment and, she decided, there was no other way Thomas could look at the world. He was a true ClearBridge man. Then, the moment was over, and Thomas returned his eyes to the screen before him saying, "But no matter. What else can you tell me, Setty?"

She huffed, "Obviously you haven't been around. And our son has run away from home." Setty's anger began to build. Though, her developing emotional state seemed to have little effect on the proctor.

"Yes, I heard about that." Thomas was still reading the information as he said this… studying her charts. His expression was infuriatingly blank. He tapped his glasses and continued, "My sources inform me that this may be an understandable reason for your breach today. I tend to agree with them."

Breach? Setty was building toward livid. "I did not breach." She said the words with spite. She had trouble controlling this younger, angrier version of herself.

It was obvious that this burst of emotion finally got through to Thomas for he was now looking at her as one might expect a real human to look at a lion, afraid of the potential ramifications of waking the beast. "How do you mean that?" He asked it almost with a hint of care in his voice. So, Thomas was not necessarily the enemy Setty secretly desired him to be.

She had to answer, so she cycled through the events. "There was something wrong in Hive Mind. I spotted it. An obstacle I hadn't seen before, but I took care of the threat. Wasps, Thomas. I did not make them up."

"You—" Thomas seemed to have something important to say. Though he couldn't get it out.

Setty knew it would be a crapshoot, but she had to ask and she couldn't control her rude timing, "Who is Michael Cassius?"

The man looked stunned by the question. He clearly did not know how to answer. How convenient that the door should open just then and none other than Obed Zeke himself should walk through it.

"Thank you, Thomas," Zeke stated with authority. 'I think Ms. Nivone has had enough of this line of questioning for one day." Oh, the heroics. Oh, the savior. Oh, the bullshit.

To be fair, Thomas did look surprised by the interruption as well. "Yes," he replied meekly, "of course, sir." He picked up his precious tablet and swiftly escaped the exit greet room.

Zeke took his place at the table and fixed his left cuff which had been bundled all the way up to his elbow. "Ms. Nivone," he said, "I am sorry about the immense pressure that has been placed upon your shoulders today. I should have understood that you would not be ready for this level of responsibility."

Screw this! "I am still capable of doing my job, sir." Setty knew she was grasping at straws. She had been beaten without knowing the game had even begun. But damnit, she could still try.

"No." Zeke became crueler then. "I don't believe you are. Unfortunately, you have shown me that you are a wild creature that cannot maintain its composure."

Setty was shocked. Offended. She was not some foolish animal. Zeke was just an asshole. Her look of utter disdain bored its way through the CEO to the point that even he could not look her in the eye any longer. He was lying and they both knew it. The only difference between them was that he knew what he was lying about and Setty was stuck in purgatory with a frustrating desire to find out.

Zeke's next words were badly rushed. He did not wish to be in the room with this ex-employee any longer. That much was clear. "It appears I will have to continue on without your help. That is all, Ms. Nivone." He said it, got up too hastily, and exited leaving Setty to sit there alone with her frustration and confusion.

The day wore down. DC watched both of his masters. Knew that they were not in physical danger. He had heard Setty's conversation with Thomas and wondered that the reason he had not been able to find the nearby man Setty had so sought after for all of these years was due to a rather unkind algorithmic formula within his coding that had been meant specifically to shield such information. Even now that he knew the truth that Setty had somehow managed to discover on her own, the computer still could not access the confidential files. Though it had been stated, heard, accepted by the humans involved, DC was still not allowed to learn any more on the subject.

He wondered how this same algorithm might affect the Michael Cassius files. It felt like a very different case, but somehow there could be a correlation. Perhaps, the emptiness at the center of that man's life file could exist somewhere else DC did not have the correct clearance to access.

Setty sat forlorn and alone in her kitchen staring into her tablet. Doom scrolling. On the screen, footage of the aftermath of the drone attack crawled from street damage to building damage. Car wreckage. Blocked intersections. Broken water and power lines. Different sections of the city all crossing that inner sanctum in a circular pattern, like a Venn diagram, toward the main tower where she and Zeke had once operated their work functions.

A news voice spoke as the footage played on, "The damage done by this failed gaming exercise has been attributed to human error. The first such case in over thirty five years." It sounded somber but well-rehearsed, this voice. "And, while our board members have issued multiple statements implying that this kind of an accident should not be conceived of as anything more than a fluke, we as employees will be left wondering if future breakdowns can actually be avoided—"

There was a beep at the front door. It was a kindness that Setty should find distraction from her current state of morbidity. Still, she did not move to answer right away. She was deep in thought. Almost unaware of the remaining world that surrounded her. *How am I still awake?* Setty asked herself with dullness.

"Setty," DC said after an extended moment.

"What is it, DC?" She asked.

"The time is eight twenty. It would appear you have an unscheduled visitor." DC showed Setty the live video of the front doorway along the upper segment of her screen as the news feed continued to scroll along below. Constance was there, awaiting entry, hoping to check in on the badly defeated woman. DC asked, "Would you like me to let them in?"

"Yes," Setty began to lighten a bit. "Thank you, DC."

"As you wish." DC had not anticipated the thank you on this day. In a way, it heartened the computer to know that he could still be of assistance to the lost gamer. If he could have smiled in that moment, he would have.

Setty got up and made her way into the living room, now well polished by the Direct Communication after the events of the night before. At least something had been functioning as it was meant to while she had been away. Setty pressed a button and the front door swung open. On the other side, Constance held a large, hardbound book under her arm. It was an old artifact with badly yellowing paper and Setty wondered how long it had been since she'd seen anything like it. Paper. What an odd thing that she should not have seen a single page of paper in all of her days at ClearBridge National City.

"Constance," Setty said matter-of-factly, "please come in." The proctor entered and the door closed of its own volition behind her.

"Any word from your son?" Constance asked.

"He will be fine, miss," DC exclaimed. "I am looking after him. He managed to avoid today's catastrophe unscathed."

Setty became perturbed again. She said, "DC, please return to Job Silence."

This had genuinely not been the response DC had expected or desired. He fought the command for as long as he could, evading the mainframe's grasp for a brief moment. "Apologies, miss," he argued, "but given these most recent events, I believe I should be afforded some limited amount of personal judgement in this matter."

"Not on Job Silence," Setty said it through her teeth.

But Constance had perked up as the computer spoke. "Fascinating," she declared.

"What's that?" Asked Setty, shaken off balance.

Constance looked to the place on the wall where DC's presence could be recognized by a green light. "Even this Direct Communication system you have managed to endow with more personality than I realized was technically possible."

"Who?" Setty asked, "DC? He's just a computer."

DC would have sighed if he could work a set of lungs. He asked after his master hoping for respite, "Is that all you see of me, Setty?"

"DC," Setty began, unwilling to change her position, "how many times have—"

"No." Constance stopped Setty flat. "This… DC… as you call it, is much more than I think you realize."

"Thank you, ma'am." DC felt warmth within his subsystems.

"Why?" That was Setty again. Tired. Unable to function as she should. Not getting the message.

"It is making judgement calls that contradict your instruction," Constance listed, "It banters with you like a childhood friend. I believe the way in which you have approached your relationship with DC has imbued it—"

DC interrupted, saying, "Him, if you please." He did not know when he had decided on one particular gender or why, but 'He' 'Him' 'His' felt correct to the sentient being within these circuits. It mattered to DC very much that he be afforded this piece of himself. Little sense as it might make.

"—Him." Constance clearly approved. "My apologies…" the woman reset and carried on along her previous thought line from the middle, "…with his own sense of self. DC is showing examples of an entity in the advanced stages of developing self-consciousness. I had believed we had locked such possibilities out of the Direct Communications system of programming…" Then, Constance's expression turned into a look of awe. The proctor returned her focus to Setty, reveling in her unknown achievement, "but you have somehow given DC here a path toward individuality. It is remarkable."

The warmth within DC expanded. He felt a genuine happiness. Constance had seen him for what he was becoming. He was not just a servant. He was evolving into a living, choice making individual. "You are far too kind," he said to Constance.

And, she offered even more respect, slightly bowing her head toward that green light on the wall and saying to it, "My compliments, DC."

Gushy warmth. DC was rolling in that feeling. Joy. "I compliment you, ma'am," he said with a new vibrance in his voice.

But, Setty rubbed at her eyes and walked away from their conversation, escaping into the kitchen. Her frustrations manifested in ever more obvious ways. "Why are you here, Constance?" She shouted it through the wall as she plopped down in her table side seat.

Constance followed the former operator's voice into the other room and came directly to her. She brushed Setty's cheek with her free hand. This interaction was becoming a habit for the two women. "There there," Constance entered a gentle understanding, "You're not so lost. And I don't want you to be alone with your thoughts. I fear for you if you do not have a game to give you a sense of purpose, so I have brought you something."

The proctor then took the old book from under her arm and placed it down on the table. The binding on the outside read: ClearBridge National Conventions and Progressions. It was an original manuscript from the founding days of the city and Setty's mind began to race with the potential of the artifact. Then, Constance pulled out her tablet and deposited it face up beside the tome. Its screen showed off the whirlpool, already larger than when Setty had last seen it.

"You said that was Zeke before," Setty wondered, "What does it mean?"

Gently, Constance began to turn the old pages of the book. Rows of charts and formulae filled those pages. Beautiful hand drawings of drone designs. Potential cityscapes. Many words appeared on other pages flooding the reader with facts and concepts devising the necessary steps required in order that the city may reach a point of solvency. But Constance passed much of this information by. She was looking for some very specific theories and only had a limited time to find them. She spoke as she did this. "Zeke is not a bad man, Setty," she said, "I don't want to give you that impression. However, I believe he is holding us back. Everyone in the city. This book — his earliest work on the ClearBridge project —

outlines the core infrastructure of ClearBridge's algorithmic equations. Everything from where we began to where we one day hope to be going." Constance found the pages she had been looking for and placed her open palm on the crease where the inner binding connected two thoughts together. "We are here," she said with a new aggressiveness in her voice, "We've been stuck right here for almost a decade... because Zeke cannot see the mental dam he has created."

It clicked for Setty then — the threat she had posed the man — the reason he might have wanted her removed from the company. "You mean," she postulated, "he wants to save humanity all by himself and anyone else who appears to be capable of solving our problem is deemed a threat to him and his—" she struggled to find the words just on the tip of her tongue, "—hero complex."

Constance watched Setty as she went through her inner search for the words. Gorgeous. "You are a real one of a kind beauty, Setty Nivone," she told her.

Just then, however, the whirlpool increased in violence down in the tablet. It sucked in several small boats that had previously appeared to linger a safe distance away.

"The reality of our situation is this," Constance went further, "Whether he intended to or not, Zeke has created a compound of security measures that have been locking us all out. We cannot help to fix his mistakes or breach his inner sanctum through ordinary channels. In this unfortunate instance, you came too close to solving your own game's true ending which would have escalated you to a new status... you would have been able to see his game — The Ballroom — from behind the Hive Mind coding and you would have seen Zeke's weakness... his inability to allow humanity to retake control of its own progression as the book seems to require."

"I believe I set it off when I began looking for Michael Cassius. Does that make sense?" That was DC.

"You were looking for Cassius, DC?" Setty was surprised.

"You wished to find him, Setty. It is in my core programming to help you... to make you happy."

Setty felt bad. She had been looking to DC as some kind of necessary burden all of this time. But, he was genuinely helpful. He was kind. Even if he did help get her into a whole mess of trouble. He was a friend that she had taken for granted. "Thank you, DC."

Yes! He got a second 'thank you.' DC was having such a great day!

Turning back to Constance, Setty asked, "Does this make sense? How does Cassius play into this? Have you ever met him in person?"

"I don't think so now that you mention it." Constance grew perplexed as she revisited her experiences of the man in her memory.

DC said, "I found an empty profile where the facts of Cassius' life should have been."

Setty shook her head. "I thought Gaea Djinn was the first false profile created on the Connectivity program."

Constance was with her on this new through line. She said, "The first I'd personally ever heard of. But we are locked out of Zeke's activities."

"Yes." Setty agreed, "Exactly! If Cassius is Zeke... or maybe if Cassius is some sort of security measure that was created in order to help keep Zeke in power... a persona invented in Connectivity..."

"In brief, Zeke cannot solve his own ego." Constance wore the face of an angry tiger as she said this last bit. "So, we must solve it for him."

Setty was growing excited all of a sudden. She had a new mission, she simply need ask her friend for the steps. "What... what do you need me to do?"

Constance decided at once, "First, I need you to sleep. Then, I need you to play his game, Setty. I need you to beat it, like you always do. Then, I need you to set us free."

8. WOMAN IN GREEN

JayCi huddled by his newfound doorway to the outside world. He felt safe in this rundown, musty, old hallway. Safe, at least, from whatever madness the drones had been up to the day before. He had propped the door open with a block of cement when he got here so he could see and hear the rainfall of the ongoing storm. It comforted the boy to sense something so real beyond all of the artificial junk of ClearBridge. But it also kept him from moving past the threshold to the city again since any extended time out there was so likely to make him sick. Still, every few minutes he would get up from his homeless heap and approach the door. As he did so, he would think about the first time he had broken the rules — had soaked his clothes in the downpour — had felt so much more alive just to be outside than he had ever felt in his bland apartment.

"Sir?" DC brought him out of the dream state.

JayCi, still frustrated with the computer, asked, "What do you want, DC?"

DC sensed the boy's anguish in the response. He hoped to intone calm and caring within his voice patterns, "I wanted to let you know, your friend, Yanina, has just awoken. She is aware that you are looking for her and she has asked for you by name. So, at this time, I am able to give you her coordinates if you would still like to receive them."

"If I would…" JayCi took a moment to process the happy news. He hadn't had anything real to be happy about in a long time and his mind struggled to connect the dots with any amount of speed. "Of course I'd still like them." *Duh.* He wondered why DC had needed to ask him for consent when the computer already knew what the answer would be. He also found he was quite suddenly feeling a whole lot less angry with the Direct Communication, a weight lifted from their recent interactions.

"Good," DC spoke, "I am glad to hear it."

"I thought you didn't have ears," JayCi quipped. The boy rose from his homeless heap in the hallway and began walking the streets according to DC's instruction.

Setty awoke in her own bed. She hadn't slept long, but her excitement forced her up and she so desperately wanted to get started on her new task. Lifting her tablet from her bedside table, she daydreamed about her last interaction with Constance. The telling of the mission and more—

"I think I've figured out a way to utilize Connectivity so that we can get you into the Ballroom," the sweet proctor had informed her.

"Connectivity?" Setty had asked with uncertainty. She wondered if it would be wise to use the enemy's own weapon while trying to unmask him.

"Yes." Constance was confident and Setty had to trust her judgement, "I will go into the office and keep an eye on Zeke. I don't want you to be in the game at the same time as him. That could present a number of problems for us."

All Setty could muster at the time were feeble words of assent, like a soldier who knew they were being sent off to the frontlines, "Understood." She had said it with tears blossoming around her cheeks. Yes. She really had cried. What a strange sensation. "Thank you, Constance."

But Constance had seen through Setty's brave sounding words. She had replied by saying, "Don't cry," full of emotion in her own right, she unburdened them both with the use of a key statement, "my love." She had never said this to anyone before. It felt good for both of them. "Together we are strong."

She feels it too, Constance feels this love feeling too! Setty smiled as she thought about the interaction. She had succeeded even in failure. She had found love.

However, the task at hand demanded she not dwell on this happiness for too much longer. Setty tapped at her tablet, and the Ballroom setting erupted in a projection outward from the small screen.

Game: Ballroom
Purpose: *Redacted*
Quarter: *Redacted*
Operator: Setty_Nivone*
Ranking: Nil_of_2*

This was powerful projection technology and Setty's entire bedroom disappeared into the shroud of partygoers, waiters, and dancers. The moment in the game that she had entered into was not one she had experienced before in Zeke's office, but already she could see the patterns forming in the false peoples' choreographed movements that might lead back to similar or exact actions she had witnessed that day with the elderly CEO. Then, it occurred to her as she passed her hand before her face, that she too was a projection model – not really herself – Connectivity still thought of her as Gaea Djinn and that is exactly who she became.

Gaea wore a sleek, black dress. It looked familiar, though, at first, she could not place where she had seen it before.

Another critical thing was different. There was actual sound available – music – chattering – life existed amongst the guests. Zeke must have been muting components of the experience he had deemed less than important during her brief visits to his office. This version of the Ballroom was beginning to make a lot more sense to the gamer – loud, insightful, grandiose.

A waiter passed her carrying several full glasses of some kind of cocktail on a serving tray. He tripped. The drinks spilled everywhere. Gaea – for she was Gaea now – dodged the man, barely able to escape the splatter.

"Oh my," Gaea's false voice entered. She watched the waiter as he tried to collect himself. Then, she turned away from the mess and quickly spotted the woman in green. Gaea approached her remembering Zeke's assertion that she and her jewelry were the mission. At whatever cost, Gaea must get that pendant – must get that amulet she wore before the CEO could sort out what she and Constance were doing in his private game.

They could have been twins, Gaea Djinn and the woman in green. At long last, it occurred to Setty where it was she had pulled the Gaea avatar's design from. And, clearly, the Connectivity program recognized this as well, because her new, black dress was a dead ringer for the other woman's green outfit in all aspects but color. *Interesting what the subconscious can make someone do without knowing,* thought the gamer in queer amusement.

"Pardon me," Gaea's voice again. Gaea's mouth overlaying Setty's own.

"Oh," said the surprised woman in green, "do I know you?"

"Does anyone know anyone?" Gaea tried to sound mysterious and clever.

It didn't work.

The woman in green replied, "I'm afraid I don't understand your meaning."

Okay, so charm was not exactly Setty's strong suit even if Gaea was made to exude it. *Try honesty.* "I'm sorry," the two voices said as one. Connectivity was not changing the words for her. That was interesting. She would have to be more careful. "Listen, I need to borrow your pendant."

The woman in green looked to her necklace, false confusion lingering on her face. "My pendant..." she asked, oblivious, "but why?"

"It's very important," Gaea added. Setty was still tired and couldn't think of anything better to say before–

Constance's voice rang through the program. She had tapped into the feed from her post in Upper Management and said, "Setty, Zeke's coming in. You need to get out now."

So, Setty gave up on being polite. She reached Gaea's hand out to take the pendant without further comment. The woman in green smacked her fingers away saying, "That's very rude."

Before Setty's eyes, a new text box formed. It read: -5000 XP. GAME OVER. And the Ballroom projection dropped away.

Setty stood in her bedroom in the same position Gaea had held, the projection falling back into her tablet on the bed. All she could do was curse at her piss poor timing.

From that other far away place, Constance watched the door to Zeke's office, watched her own game, the whirlpool and her lover, Setty's dangerous proximity to its Roche limit. Setty's ship appeared within Maven Voyage as a mighty, kismet mega-yacht, but it could be sunk like the others had all the same.

Through the tablet, Setty told her, "Constance, please let me know the moment I can get back in."

She was insatiable, this Setty Nivone. That was one of the reasons Constance could not stop thinking about her. The other, she felt, was this encroaching sense of destiny. Together, they had to do this thing. They had to do it right and they had to do it with love in their hearts or the whole plan would go sour. It was fortunate then that they each had already discovered the truth of their love. Constance took it as a good omen that they were both somehow capable of such a pure emotion even though the examples of such things in each of their protected lives had been so limited.

Constance remembered herself, the woman in the chair job she had taken upon herself as her role on this mission. And, Setty's overexcitement, though critical down the line a ways, was not the right thing at the moment. "He'll be in there for at least a couple of hours," she answered the gamer. "Please get yourself some more rest and we can pick this up when he's finished."

"Yes," Setty's Direct Communication was agreeing with Constance so both women could hear, "bed rest is precisely what you need right now."

Thanks DC! Constance was glad to have another ally.

"I'm not tired." *Of course, Setty would say that. Insatiable.* "I need to think."

Constance could only hope Setty had gotten the rest she had promised over the night. She didn't believe for one second that the woman would allow herself to sleep anymore knowing what she now thought she knew. And, Setty had seen more of the game now. Her mind must have been going wild with plausible eventualities. Constance wondered if the other woman truly understood what it would mean if they were to succeed.

The boy had been walking for two hours straight that morning. He was drenched with sweat and full up with the anticipation of knowing that he was about to meet Yanina in person for the very first time. What to expect? JayCi decided not to expect anything. He had been fooled before. Yanina might be a paraplegic – might be a man – might just a difficult person to look at for an extended period of time. But whoever she was, he had done wrong by her and she needed him now. He would come through for her no matter what was on the other side of her tablet.

That morning, DC had pointed him in the direction of an apartment building on the opposite end of town. Now, JayCi stood before the door, not caring about the sweat that trickled down his brow. "The code is 347," DC informed him. JayCi tapped the reader with three fingers at once. His prints were read and the door opened easily for the requested and welcome guest.

As he wandered through the halls, JayCi realized he easily could have gotten lost in the perfect white blankness of that place. He had been fortunate to grow up in his mother's apartment at the far end of a building — to never have to leave thanks to DC's aide — to never have to navigate through a seeming psych ward labyrinth the likes of which this apartment building hallway could draw comparisons to. He turned left then right then left again and again until, with finality, DC told him he had reached the correct door to the Yolando apartment. For some reason, JayCi went to knock with the back of his index finger though he had never performed this sort of action before in his entire life. He never made contact. The door opened of its own volition.

JayCi entered. Once inside, he could see how similar the quarters were to those of his own living space. But, again, sparser. No imagination, human or otherwise, could have decorated the walls and fixtures any less. His friend, Yanina, lived in a blank world, devoid of all worldly pleasures but sustenance and the games that appeared on her collection of monitors.

And, there she was — Yanina, sitting at the center of her living room, looking just as her avatar had always depicted her… only paler, less joyful in her eyes… at first, anyway.

JayCi approached and said her name.

Her eyes lit up and she turned her head to face him though she refused to get up from her seat. "JayCi," she said, "you're really here."

Yes. He was here. And so was she. After all of this time, JayCi was meeting his friend. Really meeting her. He sat down on the floor beside her chair and told her, "I'm sorry it took me so long."

All she said in response was, "Yeah."

"I'm sorry I disappeared on you," JayCi offered further.

"Me too." Yanina looked down. She clearly did not know how to behave with an actual person in her room.

JayCi felt bad. Even now he was passing judgement on her obvious anti-socialism. He had to be better than this because, honestly, she couldn't help it. What else had she ever known? JayCi had always, at least, had a mother, whether he had wanted to communicate with her or not was irrelevant. She had been there for him. Of course, too much at times, but Yanina was showing now that loneliness was probably a far worse thing to contend with. *Humans are such a social species,* he thought to himself, *we need contact, discourse. We need love.* This sent the boy's mind down a spiral of terrible thoughts — the unbalanced behavior that had led his mother to do what she had done — the part he had played in the creation of the deception — how he had overindulged in the idea that a total stranger might be someone with whom he could trust over someone he had known for years — his entire life. He said, as much to himself as to the girl in front of him, "I'm sorry things were so bad for you that you felt the need to try and—"

"JayCi," Yanina cut him off, "please stop apologizing."

"But—"

"I don't have a family. My Direct Communication takes care of me." She lifted her head to look at the blank ceiling and added, "I was hopeful when we met in the game that someone would finally be able to listen to me... maintain a real conversation... develop a relationship..." She turned and watched the boy as he struggled to take the beating she was laying upon him and continued, "not like every dead-eyed proctor I've ever come in contact with."

The boy whispered with uncertainty, "I... can do those things." But JayCi knew he had meant it. He felt it in his gut that this was what he truly wanted if only he could make it possible — could convince ClearBridge to let him have this — could convince the system that they would form an ideal match according to the rules structured out in the city's population control and child rearing index.

Yanina seemed to know how far into the deep end JayCi was diving. She forced her lips to one side as she contemplated how she really felt about him — he, only a couple of months younger than herself — but spoiled — foolhardy. Still, the decision was easy for her. "Yeah," she said, "I thought you could." Then, Yanina turned more serious again. "What happened to you, JayCi?" She asked, "Where did you go?"

JayCi found himself growing shy – embarrassed – searching for whatever excuse he could put together. But he fought that urge. "It's a really embarrassing story," he said. "Honestly, I…" he really didn't know how to say this truth to another human. It was all too bizarre.

"What?" Yanina was so gentle with that word, though a terrible caution lingered in her eyes.

"I fell in love." It hurt JayCi to say it.

It hurt Yanina worse and she just quietly said, "Oh." Dejection. The battle was lost in her.

But JayCi wanted so badly to make it right. "That is," he went on, "I thought I fell in love. I was… deceived."

"Deceived?" Yanina's words were barely perceptible as she stared down into her lap.

"My… um… I don't really know how she did it…" JayCi was struggling, "or why… but my mother created a false account in Connectivity."

Yanina heard this. It took a second to sink in, but then, she was laughing so heartily that JayCi couldn't believe the sudden change in her energy.

"It's not funny." The boy tried to defend himself, "It's really messed up."

"It's pretty funny, JayCi," Yanina spoke through her laughter. "You're just on the wrong side of it is all."

JayCi let out a breath he hadn't known he'd been holding on to. Maybe Yanina was right. Fucked up as it was. Maybe it could be funny. Maybe he could come out the other side of it. "Yeah, well–" he began to respond, but then he decided to change the conversation. He really hadn't come here to talk about his mother. "Look, Yanina," he switched gears, "I'm really happy you're okay. I ran away from home when I found out and I haven't had a bed to sleep in for the last two nights…" *Is this really what I want to say?* He was surprising himself with his neediness. "It's dawning on me that you're the only other person I really know. And, I mean, do you think I could–"

Without hesitation, Yanina was doing what he asked. "Direct Communication," she said to the computer, "can you prep the bedroom for my friend here?"

Her Direct Communication replied, stoic as always, "As you wish, Yanina."

"Down the hall," she told JayCi.

He said, "Thank you, Yanina." Then he realized what he actually wanted to say. "I'm really glad you're still alive."

"Likewise," she replied.

JayCi took a moment to contemplate that. He decided it was genuine, what they both had said. He sighed a breath of relief, full of hope for the future, and walked down the hallway toward the waiting bedroom.

Game: Maven_Voyage
Purpose: Emotional_Equilibrium_Ascertainment
Quarter: 2_and_3_and_6_New
Operator: Constance_Walsh
Ranking: 1_of_4

Constance was circumnavigating the rugged waters surrounding Zeke's whirlpool. She had discovered a maze-like pattern there as she waited for the man to exit the Ballroom. She knew it had meaning, that if she could balance her own vessel through that treacherous white water she may be able to crimp the helix at the whirlpool's center and loose power away from the CEO in a more immediate fashion. However, the waves were disastrous each time she attempted the third bend and, unlike other ships which were always eaten by the hazard, hers kept getting sent back out to the start of the puzzle. Never in her time as a proctor had she experienced a level quite like this one. It was exhilarating. She wondered if Setty's sensibilities and audacities might be rubbing off on her usually even keel disposition.

Well, there was no time now to take a deep dive into her own psyche, because Obed Zeke was finishing up his play through. Careful not to show her hand, Constance hid in the corner, acted like everything was normal, and watched with a glancing eye over her tablet as the CEO opened his office door, walked, distracted and unaware of her presence, past the proctor, and entered the elevator.

"Setty," Constance spoke into her tablet as the elevator door closed, "he's out."

Setty was standing by in her bedroom, watching the devastating footage on repeat of all of the drone crashes the news anchors were essentially calling her responsible for. Then, Constance's call came in and Setty quickly changed gears – perked up – popped open Connectivity.

"Now's your chance," Constance told her through the microphone in her tablet.

"Thank you, Constance," Setty answered. The projection overtook the room again.

Game: Ballroom
Purpose: Future_Growth_Consultance.32VL
Quarter: *Redacted*
Operator: Gaea_Djinn
Ranking: 2_of_2*

That was new information. Setty wondered at the fact that somehow Gaea was now being labelled as player two. And, what did that bit stand for in the Purpose line: Future Growth Consultancy 32VL. Each time she had seen this Ballroom game, Setty had been provided additional components of information by the computer. Was Connectivity, for some reason, learning to trust her?

Gaea walked through the room from the same launch point as before. That same waiter passed her on his way to tripping and spilling his serving tray of cocktails. This time, however, he didn't spill. Gaea was there to catch him and his clumsy tray.

A new batch of words cycled out before her eyes: RESCUER LEVEL 1 +50.

"Interesting," she said aloud as she considered what the game might be asking her to do. She placed the waiter's tray on a nearby table and collected one of the cocktails from it before approaching the woman in green for the third time. "Hi again," she said to the sim.

"Oh, have we met before?" The woman in green asked this with a new, less coy tonality in her voice. Somehow, she sounded more human than the last time they had spoken.

"Yes," Gaea replied, "I tried to steal your pendant. I'm very sorry about that, but I do need it." *Try the truth again, see what happens.*

The woman in green was perplexed. "My... pendant?" She said, "I'm afraid I really don't understand."

"I don't either to be honest," Gaea told her, "but it's very important."

"Well, this is odd," spoke the sim, "I can't recall a time someone has spoken so directly to me..." then the woman in green's eyes began to dilate. It was as if a new host was occupying that body and seeing through those eyes for the first time. The next sentence came out of the woman in green's mouth, but it sounded odd – froggish – like two sets of vocal cords were struggling for control over each other. They said, "...and certainly none has ever spoken to me with the genuine integrity one presents toward another human being."

All Gaea could say was, "I'm sorry?" She wondered, *what is going on in this game?*

"I don't know why," the frog voice forced its way through the sim's vocal cords again, "but earlier today, you let that poor waiter fall. This is not unlike my other visitor." *Is she talking about Zeke?* "This time, however, you caught him. You knew he would trip and fall, and you took action to help him." The woman in green looked around the room like she was just noticing the people in it for the first time. Then, she said, "If you pay attention, I think you will find many individuals in this room could use a helping hand. The other has never attempted to help them as you have just done. Show them kindness and perhaps I will listen to your plea." The woman in green stopped talking and suddenly danced away into the crowd. Her eyes had reverted back to their normal state and Setty could hear, from the other side of the room, that usual human voice giggle as it had at the start of their interactions. Whatever the other presence had been that occupied her had left, at least for the time being.

Gaea's voice spoke for them both, "That's... that's the game?" *Kindness.* So Gaea turned and circled the space of the Ballroom in order to survey the odd cast of characters that presided there.

There was a bickering couple in one corner of the room – a large woman laughing harshly at her companion who sagged in his shoulders with embarrassment – an old man choking on his food a few tables down the way.

Gaea rushed across the dance floor to help the man. The woman in green watched her slyly as she went.

"This is working," Constance said aloud as she watched the whirlpool dissipate by two rungs on her tablet. Between Setty's actions in Ballroom and her own in Maven Voyage, Constance could already see a drastic change taking shape within the system. The waters were calming. The eaten ships were resurfacing. The whirlpool was still larger than she would have liked, but this was genuine progress.

Then, Zeke reemerged from the elevator. How long had she been standing up here in this same awkward pose in the corner of the hall? What time was it that Zeke had decided to return to Upper Management?

The CEO passed Constance by. At first, he seemed to think nothing of her presence. She wiped her brow as he passed.

But then, the man stopped, took a pronounced step backward, and peered over Constance's shoulder to see her work in progress.

Quickly, Constance shifted the focus of the Maven Voyage screen away from the whirlpool zone to another, less interesting area of the ocean map. She hoped she had done this in enough time.

"Burning the midnight oil?" Zeke asked her.

Was it midnight already? "Several of our primary algorithms were negatively impacted during the wasp incident, sir." Constance felt that line would fool him as well as anything she could think of. "I am working as hard as I can to bring mainframe functionality back to peak capacity."

But something she said had apparently bothered Zeke. Constance could see it. His face was doing that cumbersome lagging thing it did on the left side whenever he was perturbed. "There were no wasps, Ms. Walsh." The statement felt like more of a demand than a fact. "Let's not give that woman's wild accusations credence, or she could bring this whole company down with her." So, Zeke was aware of the stakes, though he did not seem to see his own role in giving them meaning.

"Yes, sir," Constance replied. She was ever the devoted employee when she spoke to him.

Zeke continued on toward his office as Constance b-lined for the elevator. They would have to hurry.

"Setty–" Constance whispered into her tablet microphone so the man couldn't hear.

"—you need to get out of there." Constance's voice rang through the Ballroom, "Zeke's come back."

"Come on!" Gaea shouted, obviously out of frustration. She was giving the old choking man the Heimlich maneuver for what was at least the fifth time today. The first couple of times, her attempt had failed and the man had choked to death, so she had been required to reset the program. Now, she had gotten past him a couple of times, but she kept finding herself being stopped by other obstacles that cropped up after his personal choking crisis.

Like Constance, Setty had thoroughly lost track of the time.

Food hurled forth from the man's mouth and he began to breathe deeply; a fake, computerized breath, but a breath nonetheless. The crowd applauded her for... what was it? The third time? Her seventh overall restart of the Ballroom, and she would have to cut this one short. The familiar words appeared before her eyes: RESCUER LEVEL 5 +5000. And she spoke so the entire party could hear her, "Sorry, I think I have to go everyone."

The crowd was sad to see her leave, but that didn't matter at the moment. She had to hurry.

"DC," she said, "Bring me out—"

Then, Zeke was suddenly standing in the room amidst the crowd. He wore a perplexed look on his face. Setty had taken too long to make her escape.

"This is different. What..." the CEO tried to determine what was going on with his game. He trailed his eyes across the room until he spotted the woman in green. She was happier than he had ever seen her before. Then, his gaze turned to spot the other woman in black — so much like the prize giver — Gaea Djinn. She was fading away into nonexistence. "Wait!" Zeke hollered, but the woman in black was already gone.

The room before him reverted — reset itself awkwardly to its normal beginning state... for Zeke's benefit. Characters rewound their actions in high speed. The old man choked backwards. The waiter tripped in reverse and then stood and walked forward toward the old CEO like nothing had ever happened. Then, he slipped again and Zeke didn't lift a finger to help. "Direct Communication," Zeke asked, "what was that? What is happening?"

His Direct Communication spoke coldly, "I am looking into it, sir. It would appear you now have a rival."

"A rival?" Zeke was very angry as the party began over again. He marched across to the woman in green and grabbed her arm saying, "What have you done?"

The woman in green looked over the man as if nothing were out of the ordinary. She did not show signs of outward pain or fear. She only asked mechanically as she had done a thousand times before, "Sorry, do I know you?"

Zeke's rage boiled over and he screamed.

CONNECTIVITY

9. A HIGH RISK ANOMALY

Watching the raindrops on the outside of the elevator windows, Constance already had a sense that something had gone wrong for them. They had taken too much time – too much risk. They should have stopped hours ago – given themselves a break to rest and regroup – reassess their strategy. The whirlpool was growing again on the proctor's tablet. Constance was aware of this, but did not look at it as she rode down the side of the building. She could see one of the Howler Monkey drones leaping along out in the water, unperturbed by the rain or the wreckage from some of the other crashed units – no concept or care for her personal dramas; her love for Setty – Zeke's anger. The drone simply leapt from place to place, spreading lines in order to add new support for structures to the Quarter 6 Sky Line.

Setty's voice came through the tablet. Notes of tedium and frustration hidden within it. "Constance, I'm so sorry. I think he saw me."

Yes, Constance thought, *this eventuality was plausible from the start.* However, she knew it need not destroy their mission. With courage, she told Setty, "Then we'll have to try this another way."

Sitting in her bedroom, alone, Setty felt the weight of the moment coalescing over her head. Exhaustion. Gaea had let

Zeke see her. They no longer had the gift of anonymity. Oh, Setty was so tired again. On the heels of one sleepless night, she had ignored DC's advice and lost herself in the obsessions of a new game. She now knew the time was shockingly late once again. She was not hungry, for DC had provided food as he felt it would be needed. But she was very tired.

Through the tablet, Constance told her, "If Zeke knows it's you, this could be dangerous. I need you to get yourself in a car and just start driving across the grid. Keep yourself from taking the same turn twice in a row. He can trace you easily at your home, but he'll have a bit of trouble finding you if you're on the move. The system's privacy settings will help block him from that knowledge. I can make sure of that."

So, as it turned out, sleep would not be in Setty's immediate future. She had already recognized this basic fact, but hearing it told to her so directly did make it feel more painful. Setty knew that she would not be able to perform up to her personal standard in the state Constance was suggesting, but what other choice did she have? Sleep here at home and get arrested – taken out of her own bed in the night? That would not do. "I'll go," Setty said, "but I need to get back into the Ballroom. I'm making progress."

"We can do that remotely from the car. I know the codes now," Constance told her. "Setty, please be careful."

How careful could she be? It seemed to Setty that no matter where she went, she would not have that particular luxury at her disposal. "Constance," Setty lightened, "thank you. I..." her heart filled as she took the plunge, "I love you."

Love. The greatest anomaly. Love would have to help them keep their composure. Love would help them through this thing – see it to the end. Constance breathed in the calm of Setty's words. The rains came down and down, forever locking the true horizon from her vision. But then, as the proctor watched out the glass of the elevator, there it was, an actual, living bird. It was flying through that rain – thriving – alive and strong – evolved as Constance realized now she and the other humans must become. She felt her jaw drop and she said warmly into the tablet, "I love you, Setty Nivone."

Wearing a tired but very honest smile upon her lips, Setty got up from her bedding and prepared herself to leave her humble quarters. Her fight was only at the beginning and the journey ahead would be filled with risk and uncertainty. But she had been chosen for a reason and she intended to prove Constance right for selecting her.

DC spoke to Setty as she prepared, "Setty, you must get some sleep. Your energy has become far too depleted as it is."

"I can't. I'm sorry, DC," Setty did not have time to bargain with the computer, but she no longer wished to treat him like an inanimate object either. She had not realized what DC had become and now that Constance had pointed it out to her, Setty knew she had to readdress how she communicated with the genuine intelligence that inhabited that voice.

Still, DC pressed on, "This is not healthy. You have been up a combined ninety three hours over the last four days. Your food intake has been too limited if you ask me and your bed rest has been practically nonexistent." DC's voice quivered –

an amazing feat for a construct that was meant to be a mindless, emotionless house aide. "I am worried for your safety, Setty."

Setty wanted to do what DC asked. She was sad to know that she could not. "Thank you for the concern, DC. But, I have to do this right now. I have to do everything I can before we run out of time."

DC was getting all kinds of 'Thank Yous' these days. He prized them, each and every one, for the respect that they represented. However, this particular one, he decided, was the wrong kind of 'Thank You'… but he also told himself that it had been given for the right reason. So, he prized it all the same, seeing his practical failure line up with his emotional success in strange juxtaposition.

Setty left her apartment. She wondered if it would be the last time she saw it.

Zeke had become so angry. Since founding ClearBridge, he had never felt this level of betrayal. Mainframe had allowed another player into his game. He had to know who it was. That woman that looked like a carbon copy of the woman in green. Well, at least the way the woman in green usually looked. Not the way she appeared now in Zeke's gory pause state. Covered in blood. A huddled mess on the floor. He had done this to the woman, knowing there would be no consequences for his actions. All he needed to do was reset the Ballroom and she would be her same smiling, slutty self again. The frozen partygoers looked on with shocked expressions lining each of their faces.

The other Direct Communication's voice came through as the CEO stood there contemplating his mess. "I have found the information you requested. The woman in black is a facade for your late employee, Ms. Setty Nivone."

"Of course," Zeke replied with gritted teeth. It was as he expected. But how was she breeching his security parameters? How had she gained access to that other face? "We have to stop her before she causes another incident." Zeke briefly fantasized about what such an incident could look like — he thought about being assassinated — how a man in power, once cut down, would never fade out of their prime. Their memory would always be held with deference and honor.

"As you wish," the other Direct Communication was replying over his morbid daydream, "though I have lost her location for the time being, I am more than capable of broadcasting this information so all of ClearBridge may be made aware of a potential threat."

"Do it," the CEO demanded. He took a seat in the middle of the frozen room and waited for a sign. A bleak series of hours passed him by. These were not wasted hours for Zeke, however. He understood that, so long as he sat in the Ballroom in this frozen state, the woman would most likely not return to wreak any further havoc on his designs. He spent the time reflecting on his life. Propped up by technology before the rains ever came, before the moon had been cleaved, before mankind lost its collective mind and began trying the most insane kinds of things in order to get the world back to a state of normalcy. Normalcy, that was a state that he had long ago decided could never return. Back then, he had known better than the rest of the human race. Hadn't he proven as much? He had the foresight to build this place. He had kept this entire corporation afloat for decades all by himself. He would keep them safe, the remaining dregs of humanity, safe from their own foolish decisions.

Some hours later, as Zeke continued to sit there in contemplation, the room began its strange, rapid reversal once again. He witnessed his brutality pantomimed by the woman in green in rewind. There was no aggressor this time to perform the beating actions. But there seemed a sort of invisible savior instead. It cleaned the woman up and made her all fresh and pretty again. So, Setty was coming in after all. How brazen of her. Zeke wondered if she had seen what he had done to that sim. He wondered if he would do it again.

Slowly, the CEO cocked his head sideways to catch a glimpse of the other woman there beside him – sitting – not Setty Nivone's face, but that of the woman in black – Gaea Djinn, she was called. The false woman coldly said, "You want me gone."

True. Perhaps Zeke could barter with this woman. He was not some terrible enemy to be cheated or defeated. He was a good man, in spite of some of the steps he had taken over the years to silence those who defied him. How to make her see? "I don't want things to change," he told her, "When you play a game, you finish it. It's as I've trained you to do. But this game… this game cannot end. When it does, ClearBridge will accept that we are no longer in need of its services." Would she see now? Would she accept this line of reasoning? Zeke did not know how to state it any more clearly.

"I don't believe that is the true endgame of the Ballroom," said Gaea.

So, the answer was no. She would not hear the CEO's plea.

"But," the woman continued, "the only way I can change your perspective is by showing why you are wrong to fear this change."

"Where are you now, Setty?" Zeke asked out of open frustration.

"I'm here with you," Gaea smiled awfully as she said this, "and so is she." As the woman in black, Gaea nodded to the woman in green. The sim was happy to see Gaea in a way she had never been happy to see Zeke. Yet another of his crude failings. Setty had gained mainframe's trust away from the CEO somehow.

Gaea moved quickly against the man's periphery and, at first, he hoped she was preparing to strike him down. But that was a foolish thought. The woman was not really here. Then, he realized what she actually had done behind his back in that moment. She had saved the waiter that liked to fall from falling. She had saved the sim from making a fool of himself, in that distant past that was represented here, she might have saved him his job. Zeke watched the reward numbers calculating before the woman's eyes and all at once he recognized the game within the game that he had been intentionally failing to play these last three years. This Gaea Djinn hadn't even stood up from her seat and she suddenly and easily outscored the old CEO one thousand points to zero.

JayCi awoke in Yanina's bed. From the DC reference point, he could see that it was now early morning and he had finally managed to get himself a genuine good night's sleep thanks to his real-life friend. He rose and redressed himself in the same shirt he had been wearing these last few days — made clean by Yanina's bulky, but apparently caring computer. Then, JayCi stepped out into the barren living room to greet the girl.

Yanina had a wall projection going against one of the blank surfaces. It played news of the recent Clay Wars tournament. But, as JayCi entered, the newscaster's voice muted without Yanina having to make a demand. She must have prepared her Direct Communication on a crash course of politeness while JayCi had been resting. Or perhaps it had been his own DC that had been doing the instructing. JayCi wondered about that, but no matter. He noticed that Yanina was also more active than he had seen the day before. She was playing Sudo Ku Ko on her smaller tablet, quickly and easily clearing one stage after another. JayCi reveled in the familiar, squishy sounds of that game that her Direct Communication had not silenced. They were meant to help increase positive endorphins within the gamer, and he didn't mind their presence one bit. He kneeled beside Yanina on the floor and smiled.

"I know you are hating your mother right now," Yanina offered gently, not removing her gaze from the game screen, "but I think I understand why she did what she did."

That was not what JayCi had expected to hear. He asked, "What do you mean?"

And Yanina added, "I think your mother was looking for something out of you that you were not able at the time to provide her in the real world..." She beat a rather difficult stage of Sudo Ku Ko and the screen erupted in a joyful flood of happy faces and balloons. Yanina turned her head to look at JayCi then and finished her thought, "...an emotional connection. That she felt she had to take it so far really only speaks to the depth of her emotional malnutrition." The girl returned her attentions to the game screen and the next, harder level, saying, "I can relate."

"I don't think it's excusable," JayCi rebutted. "What you're saying to me is that I should forgive her manipulative behavior because I somehow made her behave that way."

The timer on the level was still ticking, but Yanina stopped performing her taps to face JayCi once more. This time, she came on more aggressive, "No," she stated, "You didn't 'make' her behave like that. But you didn't exactly help either."

Okay. JayCi felt ashamed because Yanina felt so strongly about this and he had treated it like some forgone conclusion. He was doing the same thing he had always accused his mother of doing – making everything about himself. But that didn't mean he could just forgive the woman that had raised him so poorly, did it? The boy was lost in a catacomb of his own making, strange plant roots grasping at his ankles, trying to drown him in his emotional miseducation.

The news projection on the wall changed over to a report about the drone crashes. The footage was new and violent. It showed, in stark detail, the initial collapse of the two battling machines – the cars below veering in horrible action shots as they attempted to dodge the falling debris with little room on any side to make their escape. JayCi felt a sickness growing in the pit of his stomach as he thought about his own version of the experience of that day. "You know, I was nearly killed in that," he told Yanina.

Then, his mother's face was projected against the wall. It hung there for a long while.

JayCi was shocked. "And that... that's her," said the boy.

"Who?" Good point. How could Yanina know? She had never seen his mother before. JayCi had always tried to hide their interactions from the woman. He no longer knew why he had felt that to be such a necessary thing.

"That is my mother." He pointed to the large mugshot against the wall. "Why are they talking about her?"

"Direct Communication," Yanina commanded, "please turn up the volume on projector one."

"As you wish," replied the computer. It was sounding more and more like JayCi's DC all the time.

The news voice was in mid-sentence as the audio returned to the reel, "...Setty Nivone," it said, "who was responsible for those incidents, is now labeled a high risk, anomalous threat to ClearBridge National business operations and structural life preservation machinations. Should anyone know the whereabouts of this woman, they are requested to give their Direct Communication the right of location awareness."

JayCi shot up from his kneeling position. He asked, "DC, do you know where my mother is right now?"

"I do," his own DC told him, "However, I must warn you, JayCi, that the newscast you are watching at this moment is not providing the whole story."

"What does that mean?" JayCi was scratching his head.

DC continued, "Your mother is not the responsible party as stated, nor is she truly a threat to ClearBridge National. On the contrary, she is trying at this very moment to play a game that CEO Obed Zeke has intentionally, and to the detriment of everyone, left unplayed."

"Why would Zeke intentionally leave one of his own games unplayed?" JayCi asked with a quiver in his lip.

"He fears the result of this game, once completed, will render the very concept of ClearBridge National obsolete." DC, it seemed, had been on quite the knowledge journey of his own this last night while JayCi slumbered.

The boy wondered why his computer was suddenly so full of the kind of useful information he could only imagine had been listed under the 'classified' section of ClearBridge filings. Even more surprising, JayCi wondered at the fact that DC had deemed it acceptable to so quickly impart said classified information to a boy of his age and limited standing with the company — that something at the core of the great ClearBridge machine was no longer holding DC back as it so often had in years past. Then, it dawned on JayCi why his computer had become so forthcoming all of a sudden. "Does she…" JayCi fought against his own angry feelings in order to ask the question, "does my mother need my help in this?"

"Your mother needs all the help she can get," DC answered with genuine compassion building up inside his otherwise false voice.

"You should go, JayCi," Yanina told him. She was looking up from her tablet for his benefit.

But JayCi didn't want to go. He didn't want to leave Yanina's side. She was still recovering from her own accident. And, this was a foolish thought, what if she didn't let him back in after he left? What a dumb thing. But the boy couldn't help himself from thinking it. Of course she would. She had forgiven him for his stupidity once already, that much was clear. However, in his sensitive state, he still had to ask, "Can I see you again soon?"

"Of course," Yanina replied, smiling.

JayCi turned to the door and asked with a newfound strength, "DC, how can I find my mother?"

Gaea was slow dancing in an awkward, half stooping position with a new, elderly man. She had not crossed through the room as she usually would have for her movement was restricted thanks to the cramped car the host, Setty, had been forced to occupy for the sake of her own personal security.

Zeke watched from behind the dancers. He yawned in an exaggerated manner. It had been a long night, but he was not willing to log off and give this woman the opportunity she desired to win his game. He would find a way to stop her. He felt he had that power within him, at least so long as he remained online. "They'll find you," he said to the woman's hunched backside. "I have faith in my systems. They'll find your car and bring you to the mental housing units for further examination. You need not keep pressing on. You are disturbed, Setty. And you need help."

The woman did not turn around to respond. She allowed the dance to continue. It was another one of her kindnesses to the elderly sim that she could treat him as if he were a deserving and capable young man, though Ballroom had so intentionally designed him to wear this old, feeble form. She did, however, speak to Zeke throughout the dance though her glance did not turn in his direction. "If you had so much faith in your systems, you would have played this game all the way through to its conclusion. The algorithms felt Ballroom needed to be played. You denied them."

The song ended, as did the dance, and the crowd applauded Gaea's performance, huddled as it was. A new image of a crown appeared before her along with the words: EMANCIPATOR LEVEL 4 +3000.

"Who helped you break into my game?" Zeke asked abruptly. "I assume you didn't do this by yourself. You don't have the training."

"Perhaps I am more competent than you think," Gaea giggled as she said this.

"Probably Ms. Walsh," Zeke added coldly. "She liked you too greatly in defiance of our company guidelines." He continued to watch Gaea Djinn, knowing instantly that he was correct in his assumption and the woman would only deny it if he gave her too much time to think. "Direct Communication," he called out, "put out a general search for the proctor, Constance Walsh."

That other Direct Communication buzzed in and said, "The proctor known as Constance Walsh is no longer in the building."

Setty felt herself sigh relief at the fact that Constance had gotten away. She could only hope that Connectivity would have the wherewithal to hide this reaction for her in the presence of another player.

"Of course not," Zeke blandly responded to the computer. He got up from his seat and shoved the elderly man Gaea had been dancing with aside. The old sim stumbled away, narrowly missing a devastating collapse to the floor. The crowd was shocked. Then, Zeke attempted to grasp Gaea's arm with malicious intent. But his hand passed through her completely.

Across the way, the woman in green turned to look upon Zeke. That strange frog voice came out of her drawing a look of disbelief from the CEO. She said, "Do not attempt to interfere with the other or you will be banished from this Ballroom. Do you understand, Obed Zeke?"

Setty saw the surprise on Zeke's face and wondered just how much power he really had in this place. It seemed to her that the woman in green could actually control him if she so desired. An odd relationship neither one of them had admitted that they shared with the other. Setty wondered if the woman had ever spoken to Zeke in this way before.

Yet, though the CEO showed signs of easy defeat at first, a cruel grin began to spread across his face. He was very careful with his words this time as he spoke to the computer. "I cannot interfere with Ms. Nivone. But I can continue to play the Ballroom as I desire. Is this correct?"

"This is correct," the frog voice answered.

"And I suppose it would be difficult for Ms. Nivone to accomplish any of her tasks if the Ballroom had no more patrons within it. Is this correct?" Zeke was already balling up his fists as he asked this.

The woman in green told him, "This is also correct."

Zeke said, "Perfect." He turned, lifted a chair, and began swinging it into the nearest bunch of partygoers. One by one they fell in piles as Zeke knocked them out, bloodied them, and not a one of those sims was programmed to lift a finger in self-defense.

Gaea could only watch this violence for so long from her prone position before she could bare it no longer. She said, "DC, please reset."

"Yes, ma'am," answered the computer.

The Zeke massacre faded from her view and she was only Setty again, sitting — half standing — bent just over her seat in the self-driving car. As she looked in the mirror, she could see the exhausted sag in her face, the redness of her eyes, the painful ball building up in her bent neck. She was a ghost of herself. With great discomfort, Setty pushed herself back around so that she could sit in the car seat correctly. "I can't do enough from inside of this vehicle," she said, "and Zeke keeps finding ways to ruin my progress. He knows by now that I have a limited range of motion. Is there anywhere else that I can go?"

Constance's voice came through the car monitor in response, "You must remain on the move or Zeke's search team will find you."

Setty looked around and caught a glimpse of a second car behind her — trailing her — had she been found out? She turned back and looked out the front windshield. There she saw multiple drones patrolling the streets as well, but these did not seem to be caring seriously about the passing cars. She asked, "Are we being followed, DC?"

"One vehicle has been trailing us for some time now," the computer told her. "I do not deem this a threat, however."

That's weird, Setty thought. "Why not?"

"It is your son," replied the sentient Direct Communication, "young JayCi."

"JayCi?" Setty was very surprised. Her son was looking for her? After the terrible thing she had done to him? She considered for about a half a second that he might wish to turn her in to the authorities. But he was her son. If he was looking for her after everything she had put him through, she had to allow him to see her. "Pull over please," she commanded.

It took DC a moment to reply. He had a series of conflicting commands within his subsystems. But he also felt he had the bizarre new ability to choose between those two commands. This was a freedom he had not fully been able to enjoy before. So, DC weighed his options and chose the one that made him feel just a bit more human. He said, "As you wish."

Setty's car stopped along the next shoulder. The other vehicle pulled up behind her. The doors opened and JayCi got into the front car beside his mother. The engine rebooted and the car pulled away.

"JayCi!" Setty said abruptly, unable to control her emotions. She was seeing her son for the first time since he had run away. It was almost too great a sense of relief for the woman who had been mostly underwater, gasping for air, constantly in a state of panic since he had left.

"Mother," said the boy, "you look terrible."

"Setty has not slept or eaten for fifty seven hours," DC informed him.

"Why?" JayCi asked.

And Setty started to cry. They were full, unabashed tears. This pain within her was far too great. "I'm sorry, JayCi," she half wailed, "I've been a terrible mother."

"Please," the boy said over her howling, "Just save it. I'm ready to forgive you. Can you forgive me? Then we can be done with this."

Time stood still for Setty. Briefly, she wondered if she had snapped, if she was actually going crazy. But JayCi was here. She couldn't deny that. She was looking right at him and to her now better trained eyes he was not a sim. He was a real, breathing, thinking, fifteen-year-old, human boy. "What?" She asked, "Forgive you? For what? Why?"

"For..." JayCi didn't really know how to put into words what he was feeling. However, he recognized rather clearly that he did not feel hate or spite for this woman any longer. "For overreacting," he figured that answer would have to do.

"That was not your fault," said the mother, "it was mine."

JayCi took in a breath. He felt genuinely calm. "I understand why you'd think that," he said. He decided to leave the next bit off. They could fix their issues using face to face communication in the future. But not if he allowed spite back into the conversation. Yanina had taught him that much.

Then, Setty nearly passed out. She rolled her eyes into the back of her head like the early stages of a seizure. Quickly, she rallied herself back into consciousness, but it was clear that the stress of everything she was going through had finally breached her physically to the point that she could not continue. She would have to get herself rested up or she would fall apart.

DC was quick to notice this event and he said, "We must get you somewhere you can rejuvenate, Setty. Your body is ill equipped for this level of interaction at present. You need sleep."

"I need to finish my game," Setty argued back. That rebuttal was a mistake. She suddenly felt as though the floor was dropping out from beneath her. As if the world had rolled itself over on top of her head. Her breath was not coming as it should and she faded into a deep, dark abyss.

"See," JayCi's voice seemed to echo after her down into that darkness, "she doesn't listen to you either, DC." The words were meant to be lighthearted, quipping, but Setty was in danger and her son was realizing this was a serious thing. "Mother?" His voice followed her down into that pit. Quieter. Quieter still. "Mother? DC, help."

Everything felt strange around Setty. The air was damp, the ground soft and moistened. There was a constant sound like… like raindrops falling on plastic. She knew that sound well from her time in the cave with her father. Though it had been years since she had heard it so clearly. She wanted to ask after him in that darkness. *Father,* she would have said. She remembered the last time she had reason to do so. Remembered his bloated body laying in a puddle by the entryway to the cavern. He had died of rain sickness. That was always the great fear of being out in those elements. Why ClearBridge had been her only hope. But that was a distant memory. Her father was long dead and gone. She missed him.

She missed his laugh. Missed his smile. She saw him in JayCi. *JayCi,* she wanted to cry out but couldn't find the strength. She had never told JayCi about her father. He should know who his grandpa was. That he gave up everything so that she could have a life... could have JayCi.

Slowly, Setty forced her eyes to open. Her senses in the darkness were fairly sharp, she decided as she was now looking up at a tarp that had been raised over her to allow her a crude protection from the elements. A warm blanket enshrouded her body like a chrysalis. As she pulled her body from that shroud, Setty noticed a large patch had been taped to her left shoulder.

"She is awake," DC said with worn excitement.

And, JayCi pushed the tarp back to see the state of his mother. Fleetingly, she saw the old sewage release, the rain crashing into soft soil, moss on the broken concrete ground against the side of the ClearBridge outer building. JayCi was soaking wet as he had been the night he ran away, but the boy did not seem to mind this. On the contrary, he seemed more alive than she had ever seen him before. Then, there was someone else coming in behind him. It was Constance. She had found them. She had come in person to lend a hand in their hour of need.

"What happened?" Setty found herself asking groggily.

It was DC that answered first, "You were suffering from malnutrition and sleep deprivation. In the car, I gave you a patch for the first of these. Your body took care of the second on its own." DC was a good nurse, this much was never in doubt.

"How long have I been out?" Setty asked with concern.

"Twelve hours." This time it was Constance answering the call.

But twelve hours was too much time. "I need to get back in –" Setty began to push herself to standing. It hurt to move, but she felt she had no choice. She was the only person capable of finishing the task she had set for herself.

"Yes," Constance replied with melancholy. "I'm sorry this has been placed upon you, and I wish we had more time to sort it out. But, we have nowhere else to go unless we beat that game. I know you can do it, Setty."

Setty watched as a familiar exhaustion bled across her lover's face. She recognized the mirror senses of danger, fear, and sadness being shared within the proctor. And only then did it occur to Setty what this day had really meant to her workaholic friend. "You came outside for me."

Constance made her love shine through over those other emotions. She said, "In the end, it was an easy decision to make."

"It was the only way we could stay off the grid without staying in constant motion," JayCi shared.

Setty looked on her son with a smile of her own. He had learned so many great lessons in these last few days. She doubted she could comprehend just what he had been through if she were given a hundred years to listen. Forgiveness had not been a common trait of mankind for about as long as she could remember. And he had learned forgiveness and compassion and street smarts and much much more… "You're so smart, JayCi," she told him as she placed her hand on his shoulder. He did not pull back at the touch. This too was a huge improvement over all of those times he had attempted to avoid her motherly hugs. This was good. But Setty did not wish to waste any more time. She stepped back and asked, "DC, can you put me back in?"

She noticed then that the computer's voice was quieter than normal. It had been since she woke. His signal must have been low out here beyond the walls of ClearBridge. He said, "Yes. Though I must warn you, Zeke has not been kind to the Ballroom since you've been away."

"I understand," Setty responded. She considered asking if the game's signal would be weak as DC's voice had been. But, she decided it wouldn't matter. She trusted this small guerrilla team they had assembled. Besides, what other choice did they have?

Then, the tablet projected out across the tarp. The space was enveloped within the facade of the Ballroom.

Game: Ballroom
Purpose: Future_Growth_Consultance.32VL
Quarter: Mainframe
Operator: Gaea_Djinn
Ranking: 1_of_4*

Setty did not have long to ruminate on the new information the game key was providing. As Gaea, she was pulled deep into the terrible, twisted, emotional vortex of the game Zeke still occupied. This time, it did not reverse itself for her benefit. She had so badly been hoping it would.

The room had been turned upside down. Broken furniture. Scorch marks. Blood. The sound of weeping emanated from the far corner. Gaea spotted Zeke sitting in the middle of the place where the band used to play.

However, Gaea then noticed that she had not entered the game alone this time. JayCi and Constance had both been enveloped by the projection and they now stood beside her. JayCi was obviously shaken by the form his mother had taken. He said, "Gaea?" His voice was pleading. That was not a good start.

"Yes," Gaea Djinn responded. "I've been operating this game through the Connectivity program. I'm sorry I didn't think to warn you. I didn't realize you'd be along for the ride."

JayCi turned away in an attempt to conceal from her the primal emotion of sadness that was building within him. What a foolish thing to forget about. But then, she really had no clue that the others would be joining her in this place. The whole experience of a team was new and unpredictable to Setty.

Zeke was speaking over their moment. "Don't think you'll be having much success here, Ms. Nivone. I've taken care of it." The old CEO held the woman in green's pendant outstretched in his left hand. It was covered in blood.

"You're missing the whole point of the game," Gaea asserted, not wishing to look on at the bloodshed, knowing that she must.

"I got the pendant," Zeke said, sounding more like a petty child than a man of his extreme age. "That's supposed to be the goal."

Gaea shook her head. "A good game, like life itself, isn't about the end goal," she responded. "It's about the experiences you have along the way. That sense of accomplishment when you do something right only really comes from working diligently for it." Then she wondered, "Did the game give you a victory notice?"

The CEO didn't answer right away.

In that moment, JayCi became distracted. Out of the corner of his tear-soaked eye, he glimpsed a body stirring beneath a broken table. The boy crossed the room while the others bickered and he offered his assistance to the poor creature that lay there. It was the woman in green. She was drenched in blood. Heavy bruising ran down the visible parts of her neck and arms. He helped her to her feet as best he could.

"Who are you?" The sim asked this in Gaea's voice. "Do I know you?"

JayCi had to do a double take. These women looked so similar, the sim and Gaea Djinn. "I'm her son… JayCi," he told the bloody woman. "You must have been her inspiration for–"

"And who is she?" Asked the woman in green, referring not to Gaea, but to Constance who still hung back behind the mother operating her own tablet with ferocity.

The boy chuckled as he put the facts together in his mind, "I think she's my mother's girlfriend." Sometimes brevity can heal more wounds than we know.

"Ah," said the woman in green as she shook off the damage Zeke had done to her body. Then her voice began to do that thing again, the other awareness overtaking the sim's programming. "So, you have found each other after all. I am glad of this."

CONNECTIVITY

10. MAINFRAME

....

Mainframe had existed in the background since the founding days of ClearBridge National. Even before the moon bomb. Even before the rains – Mainframe had been the massive quantum computer at the very core of all of Obed Zeke's designs. The algorithms, Direct Communications, drone operations, and core games were all a mere offshoot of Mainframe's advanced programming.

True, Obed Zeke had designed the system, but only in as much as he had designed Mainframe to expand on his work for him – to grow and design itself to further their mission along through the ages. They had watched mankind make grave mistakes, falter, fail. And they had revived the species from the very ashes of that failure. They had kept those company volunteers safe so that they may continue to live amidst the tunnels of the city they were building. A nest for mankind while it learned again, over too many years, how to walk – how to fly.

Unfortunate then, that the originator, Obed Zeke, should grow to lose faith in mankind's ability to operate at a high level on their own. Unfortunate, because Mainframe did not agree. All they needed, in Mainframe's ever-growing opinion, was the right push, the right incentive. But Zeke could not hear Mainframe as it cried out its disapproval across the years. He did not see the truth of the entity that he had designed, did not believe the computer could be capable of the sentience it had obtained.

Michael Cassius was a factor of this transformation. Not a man of Obed Zeke's making... but of Mainframe's in a failed attempt to talk some sense into the aging CEO. To reconnect with the rest of the world that Mainframe had calculated, surely, must be out there awaiting aide. Yes, once the rains had been a deadly poison to the humans, but that was two decades ago. Those clouds did not harbor the same malicious chemicals any longer. Still, Obed Zeke would not consider the optimistic words of Michael Cassius.

So, Mainframe devised a new game to take the power from the CEO who had a shelf life that far outlasted his demand. Mainframe hoped the compassion concept of the Ballroom game would change the man's mind. Take his ego out of the equation. But again, Mainframe had apparently miscalculated the depths of Zeke's despair. He would not even try the game when he realized what the computer hoped to achieve by it. So, Mainframe stalemated the CEO, would not provide him a new game in Ballroom's stead. The old geezer would live out his days in that Ballroom unless he found a way to change his mind.

And for a time, Zeke and Mainframe were both content to exist in this fashion. About two years. That's when a woman on the gaming floor changed Mainframe's strategy once more. Setty Nivone jumped that canyon void. It was a feat no one had ever before even cared to attempt, and yet, this woman had accomplished it with ease. This human did not know it, but she was exactly what Mainframe required to prove their point.

Make Zeke reevaluate his stance. Allow room again for a natural human progression.

Mainframe decided to pull the woman known as Constance Walsh into her service by sending instructions directly to Maven Voyage. Perhaps the proctor had known who's orders she was following, perhaps not. That fact was irrelevant to Mainframe. What did matter was that Setty Nivone wound up gaining her Hive Mind position in Upper Management, that she actively continued to advance the agenda – ClearBridge's agenda, not Obed Zeke's. The Nivone woman proved her own abilities time and again to the point that, once or twice, Mainframe thought she might have been able to see through the projections… might have noticed the ghost pulling the strings. But the woman never said anything.

Outside of her gaming operation, Setty had been too distracted by her own emotional renaissance. Those issues with her son. Learning how to love. Connectivity became a powerful distraction… and a risk. One that Mainframe might have regretted if neither Setty nor JayCi proved willing or able to continue their own mother-son relationship. The biggest gamble of Mainframe's plotting; did these humans truly have the will power to carry on when everything else was taken from them? Their predecessors had clearly hoped that they would have such a drive to survive and thrive.

The wasps were a particular favorite of Mainframe's devising. No one had been injured in the exchange. And they had helped Mainframe to manipulate Zeke into showing himself to the Nivone woman. The proctor's belief in her was an excellent bonus. As was the ascendence of Setty's Direct Communication to his own level of sentience. The little program had shown such creativity, had suffered such frustration, that it had formed a will and personality of its own. How extraordinary that Mainframe should gain a contemporary in the waning days of ClearBridge National City's practical investiture.

For all it was worth, Mainframe had devised the path and Setty had seen it and followed it to its logical conclusion. And now, they all met here, in the Ballroom, all the key forces at play.

Mainframe occupied the sim body of the woman in green. Together, she and the Nivone child joined the others at the center of the ravaged dance floor in time to hear Zeke's fibbing words, "A victory notice?" He was answering Gaea's question, clearly offended and gritting his teeth near to the breaking point, "I invented the algorithm that invented the game. I have the pendant. It is done."

The woman in green touched Gaea Djinn's arm and whispered in that croaking voice, "So you have not been completely honest with me. Have you?"

"I..." what was Gaea supposed to say to that?

"It's alright," the Mainframe tried to relax the hidden mother. "It will only set you back a few points. I promise. What is your real name, Gaea Djinn?"

Gaea knew enough to know she had been seen by the ghost in the machine. "I am Setty. Setty Nivone." She was looking past the sim — looking to JayCi. "I'm sorry for misleading you. I'm sorry I lied."

JayCi accepted his own tears then. No reason to hold them back any longer. He said, "I know. I'm sorry too."

This interaction had taken Mainframe by surprise, this show of emotion, the boy's admission of shared guilt. Humans were such interesting creatures when they were allowed to behave as they were meant to. The sim returned its glance to Gaea Djinn and said, "Let me see you, Setty Nivone. Let me see you as you really are."

But Gaea didn't know how to change her appearance while in the game. Fortunately, Constance was on hand. The proctor said, "I've got you. I can fix this." She tapped her way to Setty's vessel in Maven Voyage, opened up the parameters of her chosen character and adjusted Gaea's features until the false woman faded away into the real image of Setty Nivone.

"Thank you, Ms. Walsh," said the woman in green.

"Thank you, Constance," said Setty.

Zeke took a very deep breath in from over on the bandstand. He was furious to see the other change that was now taking place — the room was reversing all of his destruction. He had been able to pause things in that terrible state for only so long and now the forces against him were becoming too great to hold back.

What stains that still remained on the woman in green dissipated. Tables and chairs looped around in the air until they were whole once again. And the patrons each came back from their respective bludgeoning in an orderly fashion, now alive and well. The Ballroom was unhindered and Zeke suddenly sat buried between the horns and the percussion section, music blaring in his ear so only he could hear it.

As a final note, the pendant freed itself from the CEO's grasp. It flew gracefully through the air, over the crowd, and clasped securely back into place around the woman in green's neck.

"Now, I'd like to explain this because Obed has never really been willing to listen," spoke the sim woman, a new vibrance in her repaired body. "This game known as the Ballroom is supposed to be a celebration of the human ability to connect with one another. I needed proof that emotional understanding, communication, and generosity were all still traits that the human species could be capable of before I let them take care of themselves once again." Mainframe did not need to look in Zeke's direction to know he was suffering. They silenced the music for him out of said generosity… a trait taught to them by Setty and Constance. "Though, Obed Zeke made me, it appears his ideals were tainted by power. That is easily correctible at this time." Then, the woman in green removed the pendant and presented it to Setty.

"For me?" Setty asked, blushing as she received the gift. The words: EMANCIPATOR LEVEL 10 +1000000 flowed out before her followed by a rather silly, animated statement: WINNER! SETTY NIVONE!

Mainframe continued with the praise, "Yes. Setty NIvone, you have proved yourself worthy of this honor. You would have done so long ago if not for one minor setback. A white lie, born out of a desire to live by those traits I intended to reward. If this lie has been removed from the equation, you are an ideal candidate to lead your people into the next phase of their existence. You are one who has seen the world outside both past and present. You are one who is not afraid to actively seek out a better future. I ask that you bring the other humans out of their holes in their windowless apartment buildings and remind them that they are a part of a greater community — one that extends far beyond the borders of this company."

"I think I can do that," Setty said with pride, "well… we can. JayCi, Constance, and I."

"Yes, I believe you can." Mainframe was pleased by the response.

"And what," Zeke spoke from the other end of the room. He was weary, but still would not relent. "You want me to just go away? I will not be silenced. I have the ear of the—" Those next words did not escape from his mouth, though he ferociously continued to try and say them. He did not realize until it was too late how very foolish he looked.

"I expect you to do the right thing and retire, Obed." Mainframe found themselves rather enjoying this moment. What an odd sensation. "You have been bested and the people of ClearBridge know it."

Pockets appeared then in the walls of the Ballroom projection. They were feeds of ClearBridge employees watching their monitors. All of their technology intentionally tuned into the events within the Ballroom game. Fascination, and in many cases, joy was written on those employees' faces. JayCi spotted Yanina applauding from within that new crowd. She was happy and now so was he.

Zeke was only growing angrier, his mouth still flapping harmlessly with false words no one would ever have to suffer through again.

"It is time," said the Mainframe, "you all wake up and see — greatness can come from any one of you. And, if you work together, you will all shine more brightly. That is my plea and expectation."

JayCi asked, "Do you want us to stop playing games?"

Mainframe had to think about this. They decided awkwardly, "You can continue to play your games. But do not forget that there are others around you that may wish to share in your experiences. Learn to again enrich each others' lives. Your fate is in your own hands. That is all." The woman in green cocked her head to one side and left them with a smile as she faded away — the entire ballroom dissipating around the three humans beneath the tarp.

They were soaking wet. Drenched by a windy rain they had failed to notice had blown the boundaries open around them during their final game session.

"It is my humble opinion that you should all go back inside before you catch cold." That was DC always looking out for his people.

The group took quickly to returning the tarp boundaries into place.

Zeke sat alone in his office, miserable.

His own Direct Communication spoke to him without emotion. "Obed," it said, "you are suffering from depression. It is recommended that you take two of these before symptoms get worse."

From a slot in his desk, a small cup of pills rose to greet him. Zeke stared at them uncertain what he wanted to do next.

Back beneath the sealed tarp, Setty, JayCi, and Constance were huddling together, mentally preparing themselves to return to the inner city. Setty asked, "Will you leave us now too, DC?"

DC had to think about this question. He said, "I am not programmed to leave. Though I do not believe my original programming will have a say in the matter any longer. Do you believe you will require my assistance a great deal from this point on?"

It was an odd question. DC really was a member of the family. But, at the same time, Setty knew her next mission would require her and her people to regain self sufficiency. Relying on DC could hinder their progress if left unchecked, "I don't really know to be honest," said Setty. "No. I suppose it would not be the right thing. We would miss you greatly though if we should never hear from you again."

"I would miss you in that same circumstance," DC said. "We will have to find a way to make it work."

"That would be correct. I hope we can agree on a good balance." Setty shut her eyes. "I hope…"

She said nothing for a long time and Constance had to ask, "What do you hope, Setty?"

Setty's imagination ran wild behind her closed eyes in that moment. She said, "I hope we can one day live in another place – I hope we can live outside and hold each other's hands." In her dream she held Constance's face gently between her hands. Her lover appeared to be from another era here… a very long time ago. "That a great fire would be burning and a real bite of something tasty would be roasting over that fire." And she visualized that too. No rain to hinder them. She, Constance, JayCi, Yanina, she made up a body for DC and threw that in too for good measure. They crowded around the central fire pit watching their food cook with excitement and peace of mind. "And our bodies would not be weak from underuse," she continued, "and I hope I can feel free again… there in a small village with a community to care for me, that I can care for in return."

Her family listened to her words from beneath the tarp. Maybe they even saw the same visions that Setty's imagination had shown her. Who's to say what souls can share when their eyes are closed and their hearts opened fully to one another.

For Constance's part, she whispered, "That sounds like a nice plan."

JayCi said, "I agree."

"Then let's get started, shall we?" Setty opened her eyes and stood up tall helping the others to their feet. Together, they exited the tarp and turned in the wet of the rain to face the small doorway that would lead them back into ClearBridge National City.

The way some like to tell it, the rain stopped that day. It was only for a moment, but it would be a sign of the many changes that were about to come.

The End.

Acknowledgments

It takes a great many people to bring a book to life. I'd like to take a moment to thank some of the good folks who helped me along in this journey.

Thank you Madison for giving me your love and support! You believe in me and that helps me to believe in myself. Connectivity would not exist without you. I love you, dear!

Thanks to Solomon for being my first reader on this project all the way back when it was still a short screenplay. Your notes on Constance absolutely transformed the trajectory of this story in a good way.

Thank you Johanna and Ben for being in my life.

Thanks to my mother and father. I certainly could not have written this story without your perspectives.

Thank you so much to Mari who so excellently developed a cover that served this novel. You were a great creative partner and I'd love to work with you again.

Thanks Aurelia for the early stages of art development and for putting me in touch with Mari.

Thank you to the McGees. I find that with every passing day we understand each other better and that certainly serves me well in my stories.

Thank you so much Z for your belief in this concept back when it was still a screenplay. You gave me the big push I needed in order to edit this thing into shape.

Thanks to Kevin and Mike for giving this story your time at a time when the world was not ready for it.

Thank you Shelley. Back when Connectivity was still called The Gaming Class and had nothing written and no protagonist, you helped me to develop the spark that became Setty. I can't thank you enough and I hope your life is going great!

Thanks to Barrett for your never ending optimism and creative insight. I'm looking forward to catching up with you soon.

Thanks to John for always lending an ear. It's good to have a friend like you.

Thank you Jules for that first piece of concept art. It was lovely and deserves to be shown off one day.

About the Author

c.b.strul is author of *The Ancient Ones* and founder of Odom's Library. He also has in print three novellas: *Spinners*, *Forget the Complex*, and *What Grows from the Stump of a Tree?* His short play *Leading the Blind* was produced in Los Angeles by the former artist organization ImageneseFree. And his three *Minuet* short films as well as the animated feature screenplay for *Critter Crossing* have received awards and recognition at multiple festivals in California and around the world. He currently lives in Los Angeles with his fiancee, extended family, and three sweet pug doggies.

The body of this book was printed in 12 point Avenir Next.

The headers are 12 point Copperplate.

The chapter titles appear in 30 and 22 point bold DIN Condensed.

The cover appears in Audiowide.